The Sound of Patriarchy

The Sound of Patriarchy
and other stories

L. F. Roth

Bridge House

British Library Cataloguing in Publication Data
A Record of this Publication is available from the British
Library

ISBN 978-1-914199-26-4

This edition published 2022 by Bridge House Publishing
Manchester, England

Contents

Dance?

Her lips may have formed words, but the music was deafening, so he read her hands instead and then fast-forwarded his life past early thrills to wedding, flat, child, car, a second child, a house, a second car, strain, quarrels, empty looks, long drawn-out silences, distressing counselling, a flat, nights in the pub, divorce, no car, no flat, a bed, slow mindless wanderings, shortness of breath and – the tape was winding down now – death. Looking up from his open coffin, he saw that she had vanished. Oh well, it wouldn't have been worth it, would it? Would it?

Being You

"What's wrong with her?"

Mark glances at his wife, or cohabitee, to be precise – and he likes to be precise. At his greeting: "Morning, Hannah," the girl had merely sauntered past him, nose in the air. Had she sensed an unspoken reprimand? Had he intended one? It wouldn't have been out of place. In the time she had spent in the bathroom, they could have showered half the residents in his mother's nursing home – in any nursing home. Had she heard him muttering outside? It's hardly likely. Even if the water hadn't been running, she is so self-centred that the world around her might as well not exist.

Liz shrugs. "It's me, Mark. Something I said. She's decided on a new one."

"Which is?"

"Guess."

"How could I? Who's to say she's stuck to proper names? How about Precious? Pearl? Pocahontas?"

"Pocahontas is a name. In fact, they all are."

"Well, in a way. Is that it? Pocahontas?"

"Oh, come on, Mark. It's Raquel."

"Hmm. Like Raquel Welch."

"Don't tell her that. She wants a name that's hers – one without associations."

"She's got some hope."

Liz is bound to consider him flippant, but what does she expect? When Sandra first told them to call her Moira – which subsequently became Hannah and today, apparently, Raquel – they had asked why. "Sandra doesn't feel right," she had stated. "It's not me." Well, you can't argue with a feeling. Hannah it was. Raquel it is.

They had talked about it briefly, he and Liz. She was

worried, but then she has been terribly over-protective of late. He is sure this whole business is no more than a passing phase. Children, he has been informed, cling to their mother at a certain age and throw tantrums at another. Why shouldn't they try out a few names as they grow older? "Did you, Liz?" he had enquired – he has no sisters, nor brothers for that matter, and can recall little of his own childhood. But Liz hadn't. It must be the times, he had concluded, and Liz had seemed to agree. Girls today were under greater pressure. Theirs was a different world. Being an individual was what counted. You had to be you. You had to make an impact. A name that stood out would presumably help.

These are his thoughts as he is waiting at the station, having dropped Liz off at her office. The scene around him confirms his notions. People are tapping away on their phones or iPads or else appear to be talking to themselves – the headsets these days are hard to detect. Sandra would fit in to a T, creating herself online – she had got a smartphone from Liz on her thirteenth birthday, the age of consent as far as Facebook is concerned. Reminded, he brings out his own to scan recent messages – it had buzzed repeatedly in the last half hour. None is urgent. He switches to silent mode.

"I still prefer Sandra." That had been Liz's response as her daughter, somewhat truculently, announced that her name was Raquel – which, she had realized immediately, was not what the girl wanted to hear. To approve would have been equally imprudent. She tries to remember how she had reacted to Moira and Hannah. No doubt she had been vaguely positive – why else would Sandra have made such short shrift of them? It's becoming increasingly evident that it is her mother she is rejecting.

8

At work, going through the invoices that pile up towards the end of the month, she has to concentrate in order to enter each amount where it belongs and loses sight of Sandra among the rows of columns. She enjoys dealing with figures, more so than with people, and after close to six years in the same accounts department, she has grown confident in her own abilities. At intervals there is a major upheaval as someone at the head office introduces a new program. On such occasions the learning and unlearning that has to take place can be pretty frustrating. But it's a temporary problem.

If only Sandra's was.

People should be identified by number instead of name, thinks Liz, eyeing her computer – recognizing that, for official purposes, of course, they are.

Mid-morning, she interrupts her work, saves the file and clicks on the icon for her web browser to do a search. "I hate my mother," she writes. She hits the return key. There are nearly half a million matches. Some of them, she sees, refer to mothers-in-law, so she adds minus "in law". The number is reduced by one quarter. She quits the program. Time for her morning break.

Mark's train had been delayed, but it makes little difference – they are on flexi-time. Key in hand, he stops outside the door to his office and casts an eye on the nameplate, influenced by Sandra's decision to choose a new name. What if it had read Gregory and not Mark? Gregory T. Phelps? In point of fact, had it been Gregory, he might not have had to insert a T to avoid being mistaken for any of the other Mark Phelpses in the country. Gregory Phelps. Would that have made him feel that he was a different person? Hardly. Naturally, if it hadn't been his doing, it would have been spooky – as in an American film where the main character arrives at work to discover that he no longer exists. But if he had altered it himself? Surely it wouldn't have affected how he perceived himself.

Now, if there had been a job title under his name and that had been revised, it would have made a world of difference. The simple addition of the word "Senior" would have made his heart race. But the company has left out titles altogether, eliminating the need for new plates in connection with a promotion or redefined responsibilities, a practice he had noted with regret as he took up his position – he would quite have liked his there.

He opens the door. Gregory. Where did that come from? He knows no one called Gregory. Gregory. Greg. He switches on his PC and stares at the screen. Greg. Greg. His mother had told him that, as a child, he played at being a tiger and insisted that she call him Grr, whether in imitation of the growling of a tiger or of the second syllable of the word itself wasn't clear. Was that it? From Grr to Gregory? Well, why not. The mind works in mysterious ways. In years to come, as a grumpy OAP, it might be a suitable sobriquet. Grr.

That was a Native American tradition, wasn't it – to assign a new name to someone to go with his personality and situation as they developed? Is that what Sandra is doing? If she is, she's making a mistake. Not one of the names that she has picked is individual in that sense. "Changes her name" would have been. "Morning, Changes her name. Hit on a new one today?" She would have sailed past him without a glance. Lumbered, rather – being fourteen, she doesn't sail.

With the PC up and running, Mark checks his mail, but nothing has arrived that has to be dealt with post-haste. This means he can get on with the report that has occupied him for the last couple of days. At this point, the data are incomplete and some of the statistics have to be verified – could sales really have levelled out in the sixty-five-plus age group, for instance, as the tables show, given the present demographic trend? As often before, he wishes Cora was as good with figures as she is in bed. Nor can he have her replaced by someone less prone to error – not since Thad started sleeping with her. Bloody Thad. Can't keep his hands off anybody. Liz would be perfect on the job. Needless to say, Mark can't employ her – company policies rule that out. The roles of wife – or, indeed, cohabitee – and assistant must be kept separate, though you are welcome to sleep with either or both. Nor would he want to – there is enough friction at home as it is, which must be the reason for the policy. Would that have been the case with Cora if Thad hadn't butted in? He believes not. Cora is marvellously pliable.

Liz, later in the day, not privy to Mark's reflections, is preoccupied with the mother haters she had chanced upon, having decided to spend her lunch hour delving into the matter. "I may join you shortly," she had told Pam, with whom she lunches on and off, fully aware that she wouldn't. At home Mark would sneer; here she can google in peace. "My daughter hates me," she writes. She shudders. On the screen it comes across as an established fact.

Fact or not, the new angle yields fewer results than the previous claim; even so, there are nearly fifty thousand matches. Who would have thought? Actually, the situation is a lot worse. On the first site she enters, a discussion forum, there are a great many replies to the plea for help that opens the thread: "My daughter hates me. What should I do?" Most of those she glances at are from mothers; a limited number are from men. Some have posted several messages, others just one, but it is clear that the problem is a common one.

Liz skims through a scattering of replies. It's sad reading, but not very helpful. Sandra is not in trouble at school; she is not abusive or defiant. If anything, she isolates herself. And to be told that what is wrong with girls her age *is* their age, neither an adult nor a child, is no revelation. "Be patient" is one suggestion; "love her" another; "let her sleep on a mattress on the floor" a third. How would that help? Nobody mentions testing and discarding names. She quickly tries "name change" but hits a blank. Her exploration is confined to the site she is on, but it would take forever to go over the entries page by page. What she must do, she concludes, is post a message herself and see where it might lead.

Quickly she creates an account and picks the signature under which her entry will appear. Having had her email confirmed, she logs in and goes back to the page she started out from. She clicks on "Reply". But reply how? "I'm not sure I belong here" is the phrase that offers itself, a variant of an introduction used by others. Then what? Keep it simple, she instructs herself; you're not at school – and that helps. "My daughter is 14. Not long ago she adopted a new name and ignored me if I didn't use it. Maybe I shouldn't have gone along, but I did. Within days she dropped it. At the moment she's on her third name. I'm at my wits' end. It seems to me that she's rejecting me. Has anyone been through something similar? What shall I do?" She runs her eye over the entry and clicks on "Post". In the next instant it pops up at the top of the page, for anyone to respond to.

"Still busy?" Pam is in the doorway. "My, my, is that a dating site you're on?"

Liz is embarrassed. "Oh no." She shakes her head emphatically. "This isn't about Mark. It's about Sandra." Has she hinted that things are a bit tense between her and

Mark? She hopes not – she and Pam aren't that close. Obviously, Pam could have worked it out for herself from something she has let slip. Unless it was a joke. Liz isn't always good at reading people. "Well, it's back to the grindstone," she adds, as she leaves the site. "I didn't expect it to fill my lunch hour."

Pam nods and disappears down the corridor.

Mark had lunched with Thad. It wasn't a working lunch, but, given Thad's many references to the report Mark is putting together, it could have been. He had found it hard not to flare up. Does Thad think him a moron? Back in his office, he gazes at the section he had been reviewing. Like the rest, it's on the rough side with passages marked for revision, but he will get there eventually. Generally, greater precision is required, except in the matter of actual proposals. There he should be deliberately vague. Thad is fond of imagining that he is the one with vision. Should Mark forget himself – well, it wouldn't be politic.

Should he forget himself. Mark stops and turns the phrase over. What it implies is that there is something, someone, deep inside that has to be restrained, the real Mark T. Phelps, stripped of the T even, some sort of core that must be held in check, under control – though to forget oneself can of course also mean to act unselfishly. A curious contradiction, that. Perhaps that is exactly what he should do. Perhaps he should forget himself, not selflessly but selfishly. Perhaps he should really be himself.

Grr.

He smiles. At forty-three, he has stumbled on something he had taken for granted as an infant.

It would mean the end of pandering to Thad.

And that, it goes without saying, would be tantamount to handing in his resignation.

13

He draws a squiggly line alongside two of the tables he had deemed suspect, finishing with a question mark. Then, abruptly, he drops the pen, gets up from the desk and goes over to the window. In the street eight floors down, there is a steady flow of people. Watching them intently, he sees the scurry rather than the individuals. Without exception, it seems, they are forging ahead as if they had a definite goal in mind. It may be a late lunch; it may be a business appointment or an assignation – irrespective of their aim, they are on the move. That is something he has lost. It's not that he has given up, but his work isn't the challenge that it used to be.

And not just his work – with Liz, too, he is in a rut. His whole life is at a standstill.

Gradually the view below him fades, overlaid by a vision of Cora, of her neck, her shoulder blades, the birthmark concealed by his own arm. Shifting his hold, he touches it softly with his lips. His body begins to tingle.

Reluctantly he blanks out the image, pulling himself free.

But it isn't Cora he wants to be free of – it is everything else.

Moving away from the window, he scans the room, taking in shelves, cabinets, armchairs, table, desk. It's the whole lot. It's Thad. It's Liz. It's Sandra, Moira, Hannah, Raquel. He is as entangled in it all as she is in her names. It's time he cut loose. It's time he was himself.

With strengthened resolve he crosses the floor and picks up his phone. If his life is to take a new course, he has to put out feelers. He has to notify people that he is again available. He scrolls down his list of contacts, his brows knit with concentration. Looking vacantly in front of him, he pauses at one of the names. With a headshake he passes on to the next one. Once he sets the ball rolling, there will be no turning back. Every decision counts. It's his future that is at stake.

Liz has finished for the day but leaves her PC on in order to find out if there have been any replies to the question she posted earlier. She expects none; through the day, people must be absorbed in their work.

But she is overly pessimistic – there have been four.

"You don't mention where you live," the most recent one notes, "but here in Queensland you are only allowed to change your name once if you're under 18. In that situation it's a good idea to try it out, as your girl is doing. I did. I love the one I picked. Now, way past my teens, I can assume a new identity whenever I want, but I won't. Good luck."

The second speaks with authority. "Dear 37," it commands. "Stick to the one you gave her. Let her ignore you. Sooner or later she will see sense."

"Be patient," the third cautions her. "I'm not claiming that this is what happened, but sometimes if a girl has been raped she won't talk about it but tries to get rid of everything associated with it. That can include her name. If she starts throwing away clothes and things, you have to get help."

"Where's the girl's father?" asks the fourth.

And that's it.

One keeping late hours, in Australia, believe it or not, contradicting the two whose advice preceded hers – or his – and one whose response strikes her as oracular in its openness.

Where's the girl's father?

How would that be connected to Sandra's obsession with her name?

Liz shuts down her PC, none the wiser. She will have to talk this over with Mark. He had indicated as he dropped her off that he might be late, but if he is, tomorrow will do. There is no rush.

But Mark isn't late; if anything, he is early.

"Food will be a while," she shouts.

There is no reply. Wasn't it Mark's key in the door? "Yoo-hoo!" she calls. Puzzled she opens the door to the hall and finds him on the stairs. He is on the phone and waves to her. She repairs to the kitchen.

"Sorry," he apologizes, having finished. "Someone called as I walked through the door. Business. What's for tea?"

"Shepherd's pie." Can't he smell the mince and vegetable mix in the frying pan? "The potatoes are almost done," she informs him. "It'll be about half an hour. You warned me you might be late."

Did he take it as an accusation? He defends himself.

"I decided to bring home the report I'm working on. I was hoping you might be able to give me a hand. There are some statistics that can't be right."

She is surprised. He hasn't invited help for ages.

"I'd like to get it finished," he explains.

"OK."

"After tea?"

She nods.

But as he is about to leave, she stops him. Sandra is in her room. Why wait? She lowers the heat. "Mark," she says. "I've been doing some thinking."

He gives her a searching look. "About us?"

"Us?"

"Yes."

"No, why?"

"Oh, nothing. You've been doing some thinking."

"Yes." He has made her confused. "About Sandra, Mark. I was wondering if I should try and contact Gene."

16

He makes no reply. His face is a blank.

"You wouldn't have to meet him," she points out.

Mark walks over to the window, speaking to the view outside.

"Is this about her name?"

"Why, yes."

"And what good would that do?"

"Well, he is her father. Perhaps she's crying out... I thought... Oh, Mark, I'm not sure what I thought. I thought that maybe these name changes have something to do with him. Not with us. With me. She has no idea who she is. He's part of her, but he's a complete stranger. He left when she was four. She hasn't seen him since."

Mark remains silent. She pricks the potatoes. They are done. She pours off the water, adds butter, cream, an egg yolk, salt and pepper and sets to with the masher. It feels good.

She interrupts her work to face him, but there is only his back, shutting her out. She waits.

He must have heard the silence and shrugs. "What can I say? You've clearly made up your mind."

"But you don't like it."

"No. You're making a fuss over nothing. She'll be fine in a week or two. But it's up to you. She's your child, not mine."

"Thank you. It's not meant as criticism." She smiles at him. "I'll look at the statistics as soon as the dishes are done."

He nods. "I'll just return one or two calls."

His eyes elsewhere, he heads for the door.

Upstairs, Raqel logs into her Facebook account – Raqel without a *u*, because she has grown partial to names with a clear middle. Racquel, another possibility, she had dismissed because of its cluttered centre. Five is a good

17

number. It beats her stepfather's four. Her mum's full name does too: Elizabeth.

As does her dad's.

The first time he got in touch, he merely gave his name, no message. She had hesitated but accepted him anyway – how many Eugene Thompsons could there be who'd want to be her friend? Besides, she could block him if he were some weirdo. But he wasn't. "You must be my daughter," said the note that followed and by and by he had gone on to talk about himself. He'd sent a picture, too, of the two of them. She'd recognized neither. The child – two years old? three? – could have been her. It could have been anyone. But the panda it held out towards the camera was hers.

"Don't post anything personal," he had warned her. "No photos. They could end up in the wrong hands." He'd sounded like her English teacher. His own page is as boring as can be.

Today he has commented on the names she has been trying out. "Moira, Hannah, Raqel," he writes. "It's getting to be hard to keep up with you. The choice is yours, but for me you'll always be Sandy. That's what I used to call you. That was before the hurricane."

Sandy. She tries it out. She whispers it. She speaks it out loud. Sandy. So simple.

Her mum's voice rings out from downstairs. "Food's on the table!"

Sandy.

She opens the door.

Shepherd's pie. Her favourite.

Sandy.

When she tells her, her mum will say: "Now, that has a familiar ring." And she will smile. She may give her a hug. Who knows?

And her stepfather will be completely out of it.

18

Detroit

"There's bacon and eggs if you want." She gestures towards the stove.

The man pulls out a chair. "I'll just have coffee." His cigarettes are on the table. He flicks a finger at the bottom of the pack, bringing one out, and lights it. The ashtray has been emptied but not cleaned. He places the lighter on top of the pack, then straightens it. "Listen, Lauren," he says. "About last night."

"Don't." She holds out the frying pan. "You sure you don't want any?" As he waves his cigarette in dismissal, she empties the contents in the trash. "Eat up," she tells the boy.

His protest is weak. "Aw, Mom."

She ignores it. Her elbow sticks out at a sharp angle as she dumps the frying pan in the sink. It sizzles.

The man pulls on his cigarette. "You know you don't have to go through with it. We'd manage."

"That's what his father said." Her shoulder indicates the boy. She keeps her back to the table, scrubbing at the pan. "A month of dirty diapers and broken sleep and he was gone." The frying pan hits the side of the sink. She rinses it off and gives it a quick dab with a dishcloth before returning it to the stove.

The kid's head is bent forward, inches from the cereal he has hardly touched. "You're not my dad," he mumbles.

Unsure of his meaning, the man hesitates. "I am for now," he says. It seems a safe enough claim. He taps his cigarette against the ashtray. Coffee, he thinks. He puts his hands on the table to push himself up.

But Lauren is ahead of him – she has finished clearing up and pours them both a cup. "Tyler will have to stay home," she instructs him. "I may not be out in time to pick him up from school." Some coffee spills as she hands him his. "There's leftover pizza in the fridge. There should be enough for you both." She unties her apron and drops it over a chair.

"Will you be able to drive after they're done?"

"Can't see why not."

They sip at their coffee in silence. He stubs out his cigarette, lights another.

"Remember the lilacs?" he asks.

She doesn't.

"Never mind," he says. "You'd better be on your way." He empties his cup and takes it over to the sink, along with the ashtray.

She joins him. "A hug?"

He holds her. Over her shoulder he can see Tyler. The kid is looking away.

"If you should change—"

She places a finger on his lips and frees herself to go and get her coat. Passing the boy, she gives him a sideways cuddle. "See you tonight," she says. And she is gone.

The man spends the rest of the morning tidying up. He strips the beds, theirs and Tyler's, turns the mattresses over and opens the windows to air the rooms. He gathers Lauren's clothes, but not certain precisely where they go leaves them on a chair. Unhappy with the result, he transfers them to another chair, folding each item to form a neat pile. Tyler, who must have trashed his cereal as soon as there was no one watching, stays in the kitchen with a coloring book and a set of felt-tip pens. Had Lauren told him to? In it are pictures of spacecraft, robots, aliens. The man hears him fire a gun. "Pow! Pow! Pow!" When he looks in on him, he sees him point a pen at the roach motel by the stove. "They check in," he whispers. "They check in…" He bends his head to the right for a better aim. "Pow! Pow! Pow! Pow! You're dead."

"You can't read yet, can you?" asks the man.

"Some." The kid goes on firing.

When Lauren brought him home in the spring, she'd made no mention of Tyler. Had he taken even a casual look around, he would have seen signs of the boy everywhere, but he didn't – in two days, they hardly left her bed. In fact, she didn't refer to him until she had to collect him on the Sunday. "He's been with his granny," were her words. She'd wanted a weekend to herself. Seeing that he'd stayed on, it had been the only one. How many had there been before him?

"Where does your granny live?" he asks.

The kid has his nose in the book. Is he nearsighted? "On the farm." He uncaps a black pen for the robot's handgun.

"Nearby?"

Tyler shakes his head. "They have chickens."

He should have found out from Lauren.

Deciding that the rooms have aired long enough, he makes the beds before he proceeds to sort out his belongings, few as they are; his backpack, still in the hall, held them all. A glance at his watch tells him he should heat the pizza. It is gone twelve o'clock.

"Hungry?"

Tyler has finished the picture he was working on. The colors make each shape stand out. He nods.

The man lifts down two plates to heat the pieces separately. "Remember the time there was a fly trapped in the micro?" He opens the door for Tyler's, having changed the setting to high. "We couldn't figure out where the buzzing came from. It sounded like the whole thing was about to explode. Amazing that it survived."

"It hit the window like a bullet." The kid's eyes sparkle. "The fastest fly in the world."

21

They had searched the floor afterwards but found no trace of it. Perhaps it had ended up on one of the strips of flypaper that hung in the kitchen well into September.

"Here's yours." The man has shifted book and pens to the side. He slides the plate down in front of the boy, adding a knife and fork and a glass of water, to get him to tackle his food while he is in a good mood. He sets the timer for his own. "Eat now."

And the kid does.

But halfway through, he interrupts himself.

"Your name's not Detroit, is it?"

"No."

"Mike's brother says it's a place."

"It is."

Tyler pokes at the corner of his mouth with the fork.

"So why does Mom call you Detroit?"

"She'd seen some program about it."

"Detroit?"

"It was just an idea she had."

The kid gives him a blank look but doesn't pursue the matter. They finish their meal in silence. Having cleared the table, the man washes the dishes, dries them, puts them away. Tyler has disappeared. He finds him in his room, staging a fight between a knight and a dinosaur.

"Let's go for a walk," he suggests.

They set off down the road, past the abandoned farmhouse, their nearest neighbor, where once he'd cut a few twigs of lilac after a row, a conciliatory gesture that brought its own reward. Now the bushes are empty of both flowers and leaves. "You cold?" he asks.

Tyler shakes his head.

The man slows down; the kid, he realizes, is half running.

They pass the barn, which looks more derelict than the

house; it must be decades since it was last used. A circular wire corncrib at its side, a giant birdcage, is equally deserted. This part of Wisconsin is old farming country with little to recommend it, except to the die-hard few.

They move on to the Anderson place.

Having returned on his own, relieved of his charge, the man debates with himself what else he could have done, but finds no feasible alternative. Besides, where is the harm? He'd sensed the instant they approached the house that the kid had known what was coming. He must have been left with the Andersons before. He will be fine until Lauren is back.

And she? He tightens the straps on his backpack and hikes it onto his shoulder. A heave, and it is in place. He opens the door. For her, relief will be mixed with a sense of guilt, where the blame will ultimately fall on him – more easily if he is gone.

The kid, when he left, wouldn't look at him. His lips had moved. "What was that?" the man had asked, unable to make out the words. "Will you still be Detroit?" was what he heard. But Tyler chose not to repeat it.

Detroit. As the house recedes behind him, it comes to him that he never was. Whichever view you took, he wasn't that. He shrugs, then quickens his step. Ahead lies the road by which he had arrived. He will go on from there. Traveling frees the mind when you have no set destination.

Cleaning Windows in the Dark

I wrote it on the whiteboard: *in medias res.*

"Anyone?"

Viktoria put up her hand.

"Yes?"

"Latin," she suggested.

Had I not asked for an explanation? I hesitated.

"Well. Yes. Good. That's right. Any idea what it means?"

Silence. I waited, but not too long. Ninety minutes without a break is quite enough for most students and class was really over. I explained briefly.

Viktoria's hand was up again.

"I don't understand," she said. "Isn't the beginning always...?" She looked at the board. "*In medias res.*"

"Yes, in a way, of course." She can be quite perceptive. "But we only use the phrase when we are thrown right into a scene, when we get no background information." I had to give it the time it took. "For example, if the first few sentences read, 'My name is Cynthia Edwards. I was born in a small village in Sussex, where my father was the vicar. What I'm about to tell you took place in 2010, late in November,' this is very different from an opening like 'She shut the door with a bang and stormed out of the room.' Do you see?"

"Is that true?"

"Is what true?"

"About Sussex? That your father was a vicar?"

"Is that a relevant question?"

To Viktoria, the problem with fiction is that it's fiction. She likes autobiography, which she thinks isn't.

"I know. But is it true?"

"It could be."

I had to end class. "See you next week. Don't forget that there is an assignment due on Friday." I avoided meeting Viktoria's eyes. She would have more questions.

And that is what made me think of being, or rather of not being, *in medias res* and wishing, truly wishing, that I was. As it is, although I keep busy, it is without any great involvement on my part. I'm treading water. I'm waiting for a wave to move me on. Stephen's leaving might have been such a wave. So could Katherine's. The parakeet dying was too inconsequential, though it was a sort of end point and in a way prepared for my own move. But not even coming to Sweden has taken me anywhere, other than physically.

When Stephen left, it came as a surprise. It would actually have surprised me less if I had been the one who had moved out – I had thought of it at times but stayed mainly for Katherine's sake. And there had been no immediate reason for me to leave: there was rarely any friction between us after our turbulent years, nothing to make us raise our voices or slam doors, mostly because there was very little between us at all. That seemed to suit Stephen, though, so I accepted it too. After all, the couples I knew best appeared to be in the same situation; perhaps one shouldn't ask for more. Then he met a younger woman and that was it – predictably, I realized, after the fact, listening to my friends' comments.

And Katherine's leaving? Well, children do leave home, once they reach a certain age. She was quicker than some, it is true, but that was because she too met somebody, somebody she could move in with.

The parakeet, of course, was hers; she left not only me but the bird too. When she was eleven or twelve she wanted a dog, but I stayed firm. I have seen people give in, hoping a puppy will keep their children off sex and drugs and computer games and all the temptations that pose a threat to their wellbeing. It doesn't. Children lose interest in pets sometime between ages fourteen and sixteen and then the pets end up the parents' responsibility. And dogs tie you down for life – not yours, perhaps, but theirs, which can be pretty long. Five, ten years after your child, no longer a child, has left home, you are still there, walking the dog. Parakeets are long-lived, too, but at least they don't need to be taken out.

None of this made it imperative for me to move, of course, but that is what I did. I didn't like the feeling of being left behind. I didn't like to see myself discarded.

Discarded. I ponder the word as I go over to the fridge to prepare something to eat. It is not a word that I have used before to describe my situation. It suggests a degree of bitterness that I don't think I am prepared to acknowledge. I was upset, yes, but in no way dependent on Stephen. If I had no special interests, this was not because I formed my life around him and Katherine. What with teaching and housework, there was little time for anything else.

Lasagne, I decide – there is the mince I got yesterday, which should be used. I bring out the frying pan, a spatula, and oil, and switch on the cooker as well as the oven to let the pan heat while I chop an onion. Being single has its advantages. Since most recipes are for four people, when I cook I end up with what feels like a bonus: one portion in the fridge for the next day and two in the freezer for some future time. With Stephen and Katherine there was never more than one portion left over, not enough to form the basis of anything. Sometimes it simply went to waste, forgotten in the back of the fridge.

Moving still took some doing, of course. When you are eighteen, as Katherine was, even life-changing decisions can be made without much thought of the consequences. But when you have reached my age and have a job, a flat, countless belongings, it's not as easy. Although I had made up my mind, it might not have happened if my colleagues Hazel and Gwen hadn't shown me the ad. "You want rid of me?" I asked. They nodded agreement. "You need a fresh start." No one could have been more surprised than I was when I got the job and as a result had to work out the practical details, find a tenant I could trust and arrange for a leave of absence. She is the one in charge of my kitchen now, while I have to make the béchamel sauce for my lasagne in the microwave, not on the cooker, since there's no thick-bottomed saucepan around. It works, but has to be done in stages.

Yes, Stephen, I'm in Sweden, the land of Ingmar Bergman and IKEA and the midnight sun, though there is precious little of that now, or of any sun rather, so close to the winter solstice. This is not what you thought would happen, is it?

If I knew I would be staying here, at least for a little longer than the immediate future, I could of course buy a decent saucepan. I could anyway, I suppose. But buying saucepans that aren't absolutely necessary goes with being settled and I'm not. This is not because of my job: teaching English at a small regional college is fun, even if my chief asset, it seems, is simply that I am a native speaker. I do get to teach literature, but only at a very basic level. Nor does the lack of security bother me. I knew from the start that I was no more than a reasonably well-paid temp, a guest teacher. Of course, I didn't know that teacher training as such was under review, that it might soon be concentrated to a few major universities or colleges, which would leave me without students and so without a job. But unemployment as such is no major worry. I can always go back home.

So much for looking for a fresh start! If I thought that this was it, I would obviously not see home as a backup. Nor would I hesitate to buy a new saucepan. Or rather, I wouldn't be making lasagne at all. I would be making some unknown dish from reindeer venison spiced with sensational herbs or berries that have no English name. I would be talking to the natives, old women who have outlived the rest of the world in tumbledown cottages without running water or electricity, to find differences, other ways of living one's life. I would get a pair of boots and go hiking, perhaps even vanish in the countryside. I would climb mountains. I would seek spiritual enlightenment. I would…

I would? I know someone who did something similar. Well, actually I don't. But there was someone in my school who went to Nepal a long time ago, on a mission of that kind, and never returned. Is that what I want?

The mince, onion, tomatoes are done and so is the sauce. I stir in grated cheese and then take the sheets of pasta out of the packet and carefully layer cheese sauce, pasta and mince in the one ovenproof dish I have; carefully, because it is a little on the small side. A sprinkling of cheese on top before I place the dish in the oven, set the timer.

Back home. It's strange how a place remains home long after you have left it, though in my case, of course, I've been away – been here – only a matter of months.

Outside it is dark. As yet there is no snow, which is unusual this late in the year, my colleagues tell me, but it's supposed to be on its way. I walk up to the window, but there is little to see beyond my own reflection: a few streetlights, small sections of pavement and street, part of a building. There is nobody out there. This far north many people suffer from winter depression, but I enjoy the dark; even indoors I turn on few lights other than what I need in order to read or cook. It isn't all that different from how things are at home late in the year. The dark comes earlier, of course, so now there are few hours of daylight left; none, it seems, when it is overcast. It makes the world smaller, more manageable. What you don't see no longer has a claim on your attention.

The timer calls me from what has become a wordless reverie. I check the oven and then turn it off. The mince is bubbling, the cheese sauce on top browning. I take the dish out to leave it for a few minutes while I get a plate, knife and fork, a glass of water. There was a period when I ate standing up, or walking around, holding the plate in my hand, without giving any thought to why. Was it because I felt like an intruder, having moved into a place that didn't feel like mine? It doesn't even today, but now I make myself sit down. Perhaps I should root out a candlestick, assuming that there is one, and get a box of candles, but it would seem almost a cheat, like when a real estate agent rearranges a house or flat that is for sale with props, going to such lengths as to have somebody bake bread or biscuits in the oven a few hours before the place is to be shown to create a faint smell that speaks of home – all in order to highlight the potential of the property rather than what is actually there.

The lasagne tastes good even without candles.

I spend my evenings preparing classes or correcting papers – the first term in a new place is always quite demanding. When there is time, I read. Occasionally I watch TV, but there is little on that interests me. The channels I have access to focus on extreme makeovers, of people and places, and crime. Most of the programmes are British or American, so not knowing Swedish is only a handicap when it comes to the news. But why all these crime series? Miss Marple, Poirot, Lynley, Morse and Midsomer as well as CSI here, there and everywhere – can this really be what people want?

I divide the remaining lasagne into three portions and put two in containers in the freezer, one on a plate in the fridge, covered in foil. I leave the dish to soak, but wash my plate and cutlery. I'm nothing if not organized. And since I am, I know that tonight I have to write brief comments on assignments for a class that I'll be meeting first thing in the morning.

I procrastinate, though. I generally do when faced with papers that have to be corrected – and using such a formal word to describe my behaviour makes it almost acceptable. *Procrastino, ergo sum* – would that be the Latin version? I suddenly remember things that should be done. The lasagne dish should be washed. I should wipe over the top of the cooker. I should clean the microwave oven. I should wash the kitchen floor. I should sit down and really consider if this is how I want to spend my life. Is it? Has this turned out to be the fresh start that I came here for?

It hasn't, of course, as I know only too well. The question is rather what I should do about it.

In the crime stories people read or watch, there would be no need to do anything: I would find myself *in medias res* regardless. I would witness actions that seemed harmless enough but weren't. I would stumble across dead bodies at every turn or end up one myself – though not if I were the protagonist, of course. Some student or other would build up hatred towards me because she felt I ignored her in class. Some student or other would turn out to have a mother who committed suicide after she failed a course that I taught. Some student or other would be a serial killer who followed a ritual based, somehow, on the movements of the stars, or, more simply, on the alphabet or some sequence of numbers. I would hear the floor creaking outside my door. The light would suddenly flicker and go dim. Cut. In serious fiction, chance would replace the rationality that is such a strong element in crime novels – chance meetings, a chance comment, chance events – but the result would be the same. There would be movement, developments. And that, I suppose, is what I expected coming to a new place would accomplish.

Would those developments have to involve relationships, though? Did I expect a tall, dark stranger to come into my life, as in some romance novel? I ask myself those questions as if they were one and the same, but realize that they are not. The second one is easy to answer, the first one not.

I go over to the bookcase where I keep student assignments and pick up the pile I have to deal with for tomorrow. The only work space I have is the kitchen table, but that is fine: whenever I had a desk in the past, it was always too cluttered.

The assignments are brief, some three to four hundred words, and only to be graded Pass or Fail. I glance at a few just to see what I'm in for and find them a bit thin but adequate. None has gone terribly wrong. Nor should that happen: the book, a recent one, is not particularly complex and the task straightforward; all they were asked to do was comment on the development of one of the major characters and what brought it about. I get through the answers quickly, making language comments as I read them, and then go back over each in turn to point to the need to develop a claim or provide examples. My final comment is a summary: I state what they have done and what else they might have considered. As is mostly the case, it takes less time than I had somehow anticipated. I tick them off on the class register.

The oven dish is waiting and so is the question I asked myself about relationships. I go for the dish. It isn't really dirty, but I decide it needs more than washing-up liquid and get the Brillo pads from under the sink. *Svinto* it says on the packet, but the product is the same. Perhaps that is what I should have done. I could have renamed myself and made that the basis for a more extreme makeover, taking the cue from American television: a different hairstyle as well as a change of colour, new clothes, shoes, jewellery – forget my age – and most important, probably, a different attitude if I could bring that about. My name is Bond, Samantha Bond. Could that be me? I suppose it could, but it would take some growing into or else sound more like an introduction at an AA meeting than a chest-beating "Me Tarzan". The problem is that I don't really have a problem with myself the way I am.

I don't want to be Samantha Bond.

I don't want to be Tarzan.

I don't want to be Jane either, for that matter.

Was that a problem for you, Stephen?

God knows why I keep coming back to Stephen. It's now more than a year since he left and there was really nothing for me to get over even then. Nothing, Stephen – do you hear that? Closure is a popular concept these days: people speak of closure as they must have spoken of confession or atonement not so long ago. Do we need to meet in order to find out how and why we drifted apart, Stephen? Do we need to go over our past? Do we need to find fault and assume blame? I think not. I think I know the answers. Nor would I want to go back to the life we led, which was, I have realized, not all that satisfying on a number of counts.

I'm sure they are as obvious to you as they are to me. So as far as I'm concerned, I achieved closure long ago. If I address you, Stephen, it must be out of habit, nothing else. Old habits, and so on and so forth.

Since I have the Brillo pads out I decide to go over the hotplates of the cooker. Perhaps I should do the front panel and the oven too. I don't catch the cleaning bug often and when I do, it's usually when I don't really have the time. I see a smudge somewhere and end up washing not only the door, window or whatever it is that is dirty, but all the doors or windows in the flat. That won't happen now, though; it's getting late and I'll confine myself to the cooker. I wouldn't clean the windows anyway – I did once, when it was dark outside, and though they looked fine when I was through, daylight told a different story. Besides, it is too cold. Even if I added vinegar, the water would most likely freeze and the paper stick to the windowpane.

Why when it was dark? I remember the result but not the reason. Was it when Katherine was overdue – still Jody/Peter, then, the two names that we had in readiness – and I took to housework to bring on the labour? It's funny how some of the most important times in your life are hard to recall. My first day at school; Katherine's first day at school – I could list a whole string of events that I know must have been special to me but now are all gone. If dementia is my future lot, if I grow more and more disoriented as my mind winds down to a standstill, these times will no doubt come back to me, a jumbled set of memories that will make perfect sense to me if not to anybody else. For now, they're gone. Too bad bad moments make more of a lasting impact.

You were the cause of some of those, Stephen, but that's all water under the bridge.

33

The cooker, I know, has wheels at the back. I ease it off the floor and pull it out; I might as well clean the back and sides and the space where it stands now that I've started.

There. Done.

I turn off all the lights in the kitchen except the one above the cooker. The tiles behind it sparkle. As always, there's something deeply satisfying about housework even though you know that the effect won't last. The smell of soap from newly washed floors; the smell of freshly laundered clothes as you take them out of the tumble dryer or as you iron them – these are what real estate agents should use along with the lingering smell of baking in order to hook prospective buyers. It may not always do the trick – Stephen was never one to notice the work I put into the place – but with most people I'm sure it would.

I fill the electric kettle for a cup of tea to end the day. It is the only gadget I have bought since I came here and that only a few days after I moved in. Was I more optimistic then? Perhaps I should look for a thick-bottomed saucepan too; what harm would it do? If the teacher training programme goes, it won't be overnight. I might even try and find a candlestick. Brushed stainless steel would be nice; it would reflect the light without a glare, both soft and bright at the same time. I know I saw some Danish ones I liked, a very long time ago – in Sheffield, of all places – and something similar might be available here.

The kettle switches off. As I get up to make the tea, I glance towards the window and see soft snowflakes whirling by, some motionless, suspended momentarily, some even floating upwards, defying gravity. I walk over and look out. The ground is covered with a thin layer of snow, as if it was Christmas already and not merely November. I feel a tingle of childish anticipation, at the same time as I'm aware that no Christmas ever quite came up to my expectations. Perhaps it will this year. Perhaps it will be the start of something new.

Going on Eighty-Six

"Sixty-five, going on eighty-six." Gordon has raised his glass. He must be about to end his speech.

Someone laughs, but John can't see the joke. He is still tense though the evening is coming to a close. He has never enjoyed formal dinners. They should have let him just retire.

"Seriously, John." Gordon straightens his face; he is all business. "According to the IRS, when you've reached sixty-five, you can expect to live another twenty-one years. Twenty-one years!" He pummels the air for emphasis and spills some of his wine. "But it doesn't end there. When those twenty-one years are up and you're eighty-six, your birthday brings another bonus: seven more years. And the same thing happens at ninety-three. The new dividend is four and a half. It goes on and on. By the time you're ninety-seven, you will have qualified for another three and a half. When you're a hundred, you can count on three more. It never stops. The longer you live, the older you get to be."

Gordon beams at him, in spite of the somewhat trite conclusion. As the firm's accountant, he delights in figures. "Here's to a long and happy retirement," he says. "Cheers."

John suspects he is being taken for a ride, but the string of numbers has him confused. "Cheers," he echoes. "Thank you." He should add something witty, but what? Then Harry and Brendan start singing and Jane joins in and there is no need – all he has to do is swing his glass back and forth. He isn't sure who the jolly good fellow is, he or Gordon, but it doesn't matter. Everyone is happy.

Being jolly has rarely agreed with him and so, the next morning, as he moves his legs over the side of the bed, he has to lean forward, momentarily nauseous. He closes his eyes. Then he opens them again. His toenails come into focus. They could do with cutting. Should he? No. There must be more important things to do, today of all days, than trim his nails. Tomorrow will do. He has all the time in the world.

Or does he?

"Going on eighty-six," Gordon had said, making it sound like a promise. It wasn't, of course – why hadn't he realized that last night? Nor was it a prediction. The figures Gordon had reeled off, if they had any basis at all, must have been averages and as such not very meaningful. He could die tomorrow. He could die today.

Go get the nail clippers. It is his mother's voice he hears and the tone is the same as when he was eleven and she told him to make sure his underwear was clean at all times – you never knew what might happen. He could get run over on the way to school. The classroom ceiling might collapse. A meteor might fall on him. And when the ambulance arrived, after aeons of intolerable pain – did he know that word? – and the crew eased him onto the stretcher, they would suddenly stop: "Did anyone check his underpants?" They would fumble with the buckle of his belt. There would be a look of disgust. "Uh-uh. I'm sorry. No hospital for you, I'm afraid."

He isn't eleven any more, though, and cannot be shamed into cutting his nails. But the thought of death stays with him. He stares at his feet. The discoloured nails, the hardened skin on big toes and heels, the very shape of the four smaller toes on each foot, so thin between the rough joints, offer a perfect image of decay, a sharp reminder of mortality. He has been aware of ageing before, naturally, of what it does to the body, but in a less personal way, as if it didn't really concern him. Now he feels that it does.

He gets washed and dressed. As he shaves before the bathroom mirror, death stares him in the eye.

It's not a pretty sight.

He has to get some food inside of him but hesitates: he isn't sure he will be able to keep it down. Tea, he thinks. A boiled egg. Toast.

Somewhat queasy, though he left out both egg and toast, or maybe for that reason, he passes the rest of the morning, and in fact much of the day, in a more aimless fashion than normal. He can't decide what to do. There must have been other occasions when he simply sauntered from room to room, picking up a paper here, a remote control there, putting them down somewhere else, without being bothered in the least. Until it struck him that his time was limited, it didn't matter much what use he made of it. That had been true for retirement as well. He would do what suggested itself. He might potter about. He might read or sleep or watch TV. He might go for walks. He would be his own master – and a pretty lenient one at that. Death had had no real presence in his life. But now he suddenly feels accountable. One day he will be clocking out. He has to decide what to do with the rest of his life.

It is like being a teenager all over again.

You can't sleep till all hours, you know.

Again he hears his mother's voice. Confused, he looks up. He has nodded off, slumped down on the sofa.

Don't expect me to provide for you.

The phrases, well-worn clichés, have a sharp ring even after all these years.

Obviously it must have been hard for her, bringing him up on her own, especially when he was fifteen, sixteen. He could have been more focused. He could have tried harder. In point of fact, when he finally got a job as an office boy, it was through no effort of his own and the same was true when he was taken on, eventually, as trainee draughtsman.

Still, he had made up for it. Instead of leaving home as others did, he had stayed put, paying part of the rent and household expenses. The arrangement had suited him, too. Living with his mother was both easier and cheaper than finding a new place and furnishing it. And the job, however accidental, had turned out all right. Unlike so many others, it had become more interesting over the years rather than less thanks to the introduction of computer programs.

Was sixty-five perhaps too early for retirement?

His mother had retired at sixty but had been granted no twenty-one years: she was only sixty-seven when she died. Nor had she worried, seemingly, about how she spent her time. She had been on the go from morning till night, cleaning, cooking, shopping, calling on people in the neighbourhood. When he came home from work, she would chat about the day's events, bargains she had come across, who among her friends had a cold or worse. Her own illness, the cancer that killed her, she never talked about. Had she remained healthy, she would undoubtedly have gone on living the same life until the end. She had kept busy. She had appeared content.

He gets up from the sofa. The afternoon is nearly gone. He should prepare a proper meal.

The notion that he is accountable for how he occupies himself stays with him, but gradually he lowers his ambitions. What he decides to do doesn't have to be momentous. And so, on the third day of his new life, he trims his nails; the delay indicates that it's not his top priority. He rubs the heels and soles of his feet with a pumice stone. Death disappears backstage. As he looks in the mirror, it is himself he sees.

"You're doing fine," he declares. "Not great, but fine."

There are moments when he stops in his tracks. On the

39

first Saturday, as part of his weekly routine, he brings out the ironing board, plugs in the iron, switches on the radio – he has some seven, eight shirts to see to. Then he stops himself. Why? When will he ever have to wear an ironed shirt? Come to that, when will he have to wear a shirt at all? He could save money, time and effort by putting on a tracksuit. Or else he could do what people did when he was a child: change his shirt once a week, socks and underwear twice. That would free quite a few hours.

Time isn't a problem, though – he has no backlog of work to catch up on. Besides, it must be healthier, surely, to put on clean clothes every day – or is that just what is drilled into you to keep up the sale of detergents? He looks at the pile of laundry at his side. Shirts both feel and look better ironed, he decides – though that view too could be the result of clever marketing. Has he been tricked ever since he was – how old? five? six? seven? Probably, he thinks. But would a wrinkled, unwashed life have been more fulfilling? He dismisses the question. He is sixty-five. It is a bit late to become a hippie. He lifts the iron, presses the button. It hisses.

There is timely applause from the radio. He smiles to himself. It is tuned to a commercial station.

Later, he calls David. It's not their regular night, which he missed, somehow. Since David is also retired, it should make little difference.

"Feel like a pint?"

"I thought you'd gone off to Ibiza to celebrate."

David is clearly offended. John has never in his life been to Ibiza, nor would he go abroad on the spur of the moment. Well, David could have called him. He had been at home, hadn't he?

"I'm back," he says, pretending to take the comment as

a joke. "The place isn't what it's cracked up to be. Not a drugged teenager in sight. I took the next plane home."

His reward is a forced chuckle.

"How about it?" he asks.

But David has other plans for the evening. He doesn't say what they are.

"See you next week, then?"

"Right."

The word is so lacking in expression that it can only mean the opposite. John curses himself. David is hurt. Of course, their evening out, which started as just that, an evening out, soon developed into a tradition, though neither of them treats it as such; even now, two or three years into David's retirement, they call each other every Friday to make sure they are both free. It's not in order to talk particularly; at work they had been colleagues rather than friends and now what little they say over their beer is of a general nature. Apparently David also likes to keep it that way. Being there is enough. Or was. Judging by David's reaction, being there might well be over.

He'd better call him again.

John lifts the receiver. He is about to press the recall button when he changes his mind. David will need a day or two to get over feeling hurt. A call right now might just make matters worse.

How stupid of him to forget! It is as if he didn't care. But he would definitely miss the pub with its dim, soft lighting, which gives the brown woodwork such a welcoming reddish tone. He would miss the smell of beer, the groups of people, never quite the same, forming and reforming, sometimes quiet, sometimes a little on the lively side. Sitting there at one of the small round tables is like being at the theatre or watching the making of a film. As a matter of fact, he would miss David too, he realizes.

Although they are no more than extras in the pub as well as in each other's life, they at least serve that function.

Instead of calling David, running the risk of either of them saying things they might regret, he decides to send him a postcard. Needless to say, it should come from Ibiza and the Internet provides what he is looking for: a view of Ibiza Town, from the sea. He downloads it, no doubt illegally, and opens it in his photo editor so he can change the size and add *"Greetings from Ibiza"* in white, again illegally, across the uniformly blue sky. He prints it out. It looks professional. He is pleased with himself: being even minimally creative by means of a computer feels a little like being back in the office. Well, he could have stayed on. "Can't say I wish you were here," he scribbles on the back. "See you on Friday." He adds his signature. Had he collected stamps as a child he might have risked using one of General Franco. As it is, the safer choice, a British postage stamp, will have to do: he chooses one featuring a formerly homeless pet watched over by the silhouetted Queen.

The days go by. David shows up on the Friday, a little late to make a point, but if there is tension between them it is soon gone. Neither of them refers to the postcard John sent. They drink their beer. They comment briefly on John's retirement party, which, John says, was much like David's, three years ago. David corrects him: four. It's amazing, they say, how time flies. They raise their glasses: "Cheers."

And it does: time flies. At first, this isn't all that apparent. For a month or two, as John wakes up, the day seems to extend itself before him, much like his summer holidays when he was a child, an uninterrupted stretch. The mornings, he decides, will be ideal for exercise. He considers swimming, but knows he would feel uncomfortable, as he did as a teenager, showering and changing in public, so to speak. Walking will provide enough exercise. There are places he hasn't visited in almost fifty years, which is an added incentive. As it turns out, they bring back memories he didn't know he had: the common, where he picked overripe blackberries one warm September morning with a girl – Susan? Jill? Kim? – who was the one who had suggested it; although he sees her face before him, her hands as well as his stained purple, he thinks of her, he realizes, automatically, as no longer alive, it is so long ago; the Sports Centre, where he makes out only himself high up in a tree, surveying half the world. Was there no one with him? He eyes the trunks, much thicker now, takes in the distance to the lowest branch. He would have to return with different shoes if he were to venture to climb them again. But he doesn't. Instead his walks end up first shorter and then less frequent: from five days a week he is soon down to three, then two, and then, without any decision really on his part, none. It has become obvious to him that they take far too long. When he gets home, it is already midday, more or less, and most of the day's work remains to be done.

What that involves is mainly shopping, cooking, cleaning, which somehow fills more hours than it did in the past. Has he slowed down simply because he is no longer in a rush? He thinks not, but it is hard to tell. One difference he is aware of is that he has started to economize, conscious of the fact that his income has been reduced. It may not be strictly necessary, but what harm can it do? "Watch the pennies," his mother used to say as she brought out her purse to pay, which as a boy he understood literally. Now he compares prices, taking note of special offers, and often stops at three shops or more to pick up the ingredients for the most basic meal. There is a benefit: it gives him exercise as well, so the hours are not at all wasted. And he does have the evenings to himself, when he can relax and watch TV or read. In general, life as a pensioner agrees with him.

This is Gordon's comment too when they run into each other, some two years – can it be that already? – into John's retirement.

"It is," says John. "Nearly three, actually."

"So what's the secret?" asks Gordon. "Some newfound interest? Travelling? Exploring new parts of the world? Or is it women? New exciting relationships? Tell me. I have a few years to go, but one day I'll be there."

John is embarrassed. "Well, nothing, really." He makes a face. "I suppose I live my life much as I did before. Except that I don't work."

"And you don't miss it."

John hesitates. It's not a question he has asked himself of late. His routines are well established. His days are pretty full. He goes on seeing David once a week. There isn't room for much more. "I can't say that I do," he says. "But in view of the forty odd years you promised me, I suppose I could spare a few months if you should need help at the office."

Gordon smiles. "Those figures were just averages. I'll talk to the man, though. Take care." And he is gone.

Talk to the man. At first John thinks it is his former employer Gordon has in mind and panics. Did he take him seriously? Then he smiles as well. He gets the joke – or thinks he does. He needn't worry. There will be no one contacting him from the office. His retirement is for life.

He checks his list to see where he was heading when Gordon appeared and then crosses the street. There are still a few things he needs for tonight's supper.

Director's Cut

He wakes to voices. There is no light, no air. He knows he must be dreaming. Tense, he listens, but can make out no more than a phrase or two.

"Long overdue," someone declares. "It had become quite an obsession."

And Nick Crawley, his arch-enemy, joins in, venomous: "Can't fool the Grim Reaper."

Hawkins shifts his weight, attempting to sit up. His head and left knee hit something. He is not in bed. Both arms are pinned to his sides by coarse fabric. A shroud, he assumes. He is in a coffin.

Soundlessly he yells for help.

Those present go on chattering.

"What caused it?"

"A stroke, I heard."

So he is dead. This is what it amounts to, being shut out, a solitary listener, exposed to what is going on but denied contact, vision, voice.

A man of such great promise.

There is a sudden hush, as a familiar sound rises above the rest, that of an old man clearing his throat.

"William's last wish," he wheezes, "was to leave with a bang." He lets the silence build. "The gunpowder will ensure that he does."

He is tapping on the lid.

"This will be some cremation!"

It is his father's voice.

The tapping grows louder, increasingly violent. There is a crash and light seeps in.

Hawkins shuts his eyes and as he opens them, the lid that held him down is gone and above him is the ceiling of his bedroom. He stares at it for a moment. It was a dream, as he had realized from the beginning. His feet search for the floor. Still shaken, he seeks to recall what occurred, but it is all a blur. What remains is the phrase, "This will be some cremation." Now, the coffin is easy to account for – his has been in the house for close on five weeks – but his father, dead nearly two decades? What was he doing there? Years have elapsed since Hawkins last gave him a thought. He shivers. Well, luckily he doesn't have him to contend with. How he spends his life is his business. He heads for the bathroom. It is the morning of the day he has been waiting for.

"Morbid," had been Debra's comment when he introduced his plan, but then, she is less than half his age and funerals are not, for her, on the agenda – her parents are ten, fifteen years his junior. Thankfully, that had not been the response of J. W. Wright & Son.

"Can I help you?" The man crossing the reception area as Hawkins entered had had his sleeves pushed up towards the elbow, papers flapping between thumb and forefinger. Hawkins had made no appointment, presuming none was necessary. He had explained that he had come about a funeral and was directed to a desk with a computer and a phone; a few chairs were grouped in front of it. "Be with you in a minute, sir."

The man was back sooner than that, no longer in his shirtsleeves but wearing a dark jacket. They shook hands, exchanging names, and Parker, no son, sat down behind the desk. He adjusted the position of the keyboard. "Whose funeral did you wish to attend?"

"I really have no say in the matter." Hawkins had smiled.

Parker had looked him over. "I see," he had said. But as he continued, it was evident that he didn't. "What's the name of the deceased?"

Hawkins had thought it best to interrupt him. "There isn't one as yet." And he had told Parker that it was his own

46

arrangements he wanted to go over. "I've taken leave of a number of people recently, and... well, it set me thinking." He had stopped.

He could have gone on. Three friends and an elderly aunt had passed away in as many weeks and in each instance the ceremony that followed had been so bland that he could not recall one word as he returned to his car, not one image. These people, two of them dear to him, had each shared a space with him for close to an hour but had been allowed no presence at the event. It had left him downhearted. When it was his turn, he wanted to be there.

A mock funeral, he had conjectured, would make it easier to avoid the worst pitfalls. It was a logical step. With weddings, people generally hold a rehearsal a day or two in advance – in spite of the fact that very few weddings are for life. There, if anything goes wrong, you can improve on it the next time around – or the time after that. Practice makes perfect. But with funerals you only have the one shot. That can have tragic consequences.

But why advise Parker?

"We have a brochure," the man informed him.

Hawkins had already flicked through it.

"I want it at home," he had stated. "Most of it I can manage myself, but I'll need an undertaker to prepare the body and deliver it. And I want a coffin. It would feel strange without one."

"It's not strictly required," Parker had noted. "But let's start from the top: your name, date of birth and so on."

Hawkins had nodded. This was going well. He had foreseen opposition. It might be that, like him, they'd had their fill of deaths of late. With an ageing population, that was a plausible development.

His had stayed with him. But that was a misstatement: it was his funeral that had been troubling him, not reflections on death. Choosing a coffin had ended up a tricky business. They were available in countless shapes and styles. With some, the top half opened, independent of the bottom section, to display part of the body; others resembled pulpits, desks or kayaks – or elongated hat boxes or cases for musical instruments. Handles were apparently optional. Some were decorated with religious motifs, others with floral designs or landscapes. A great many came in a profusion of materials, ranging from cardboard to bamboo to banana leaf. What he had settled for, finally, was a conventional wooden coffin, white, without ornamentation. But he kept on wondering: Is this me?

And that was just one of the many decisions he had to make.

Confronted with it, Debra had been noncommittal. Hearing her key in the door, he had reached for a cigarette. The lighter had produced a weak flame. Three or four puffs were followed by a deep pull. He had exhaled. Relax, he had instructed himself. Why so tense?

"I'm in here," he had called out.

Debra had tripped past it, as if it weren't there. Of course, once it was raised off the floor, it would have a greater impact.

"Got one for me?" She had indicated the packet.

"You quit," he had reminded her.

"I'm well aware of that."

Lighting one, she had coughed.

"Is that what I think it is?"

She had coughed again.

Her question required no answer. "I mentioned I'd have it sent over."

"Are you planning to lie in it?"

"I haven't decided. Getting out might be a bit awkward."

She had crunched her cigarette, not making the remark he half expected.

"Well, it can't stay here."

"I know."

As she departed, she had eased the door to without a sound.

It had opened almost immediately, showing part of her face.

"You should also quit," she had told him. This time it clicked shut.

He had registered the fact anew: the glow in her eyes was diminishing. It used to light up the room.

Alone, he had got to his feet to inspect the coffin, ashtray in hand.

Cremation – he had stubbed out his cigarette – cremation had been his choice. A secular ceremony followed by cremation. In fact, he would have preferred that too at home – in the garden, say. Would it be allowed? He hadn't thought to ask. If it was prohibited, given the rules and regulations these days, it might be possible to have an empty coffin dispatched to the crematorium and hide the body until some festivity occurred where a bonfire wouldn't be incongruous. Late on Guy Fawkes Night, Lester and Todd, both cub scouts when he left them in their mother's care some twenty years ago, could help Debra light the pyre by rubbing two sticks together. Except they wouldn't. He had tried to stay in touch, having his PA send them graduation gifts and, in Todd's case, presents both at his wedding and at the birth of the two girls, but these had gone unacknowledged. Through no fault of his own, his fatherhood had ended with his and Alison's divorce. Neither was likely to offer their services.

Nor would Alison herself or Barbara.

Nonetheless, he would like to see them there.

Hawkins had pictured the scene, using the coffin as a prop.

His immediate family – wife, two ex-wives, sons, one daughter-in-law, twin grandchildren – would group themselves together. Who could bear a grudge on such occasions? Presumably they would turn up in black, as a matter of course, which didn't please him. He would have to do something about that. Surviving relatives and in-laws would cluster near the doorway, blocking it. In his mind, he beckoned them on to make room for some friends and business associates – those who might outlive him. Not Crawley, if he did. Adding a wheelchair, a feasible auxiliary, but giving it no occupant, he had pushed it up towards the coffin. Chairs had scraped loudly as people took their seats. A handbag dropped to the floor; a cane joined it. The room was packed. Might an open-air ceremony be more convenient? A marquee in the garden might be ideal, unless the proceedings had to be held in the dead of winter.

He had frowned. Crowds never bothered him; the problem wasn't really shortage of space but that the scene, similar to the funerals he had attended lately, lacked life. The whole set-up was stiff. His wife and ex-wives could have been extras, brought in for the nonce. They could have been dummies, on loan from some dressmaker's shop: no words passed their lips. That applied to everyone present. The coffin itself, beyond their pale faces, their dark clothes, was featureless. What was missing was motion, colour, sound.

In a split second he had cleared the stage, leaving nothing but the coffin. Debra could have chairs, sofas, tables stacked in the garage – or maybe not. It might be safer to leave the cars in the garage and place the furniture in the drive. Vandals might be tempted to scratch a Jag or an Audi but rule a coffee table to be beneath them. It would bear thinking about.

Starting afresh with the room empty, he admitted the mourners anew, making sure they circulated. Groups formed and reformed. Newcomers introduced themselves to each other; old acquaintances delved into the past. This was better. Scanning the scene, he saw that one or two of them held glasses in their hands, as if this were a cocktail party. That had to be stopped. He began to collect them but shrugged. Why not? Accepting the drinks, he brought in a buffet, added a waiter, light refreshments. The conversation got louder. And louder.

He tried to hush them, but to no avail. They were completely out of order. "Come on," he begged. "Where am I in this?" He might as well not be dead.

He had to give them something to do, he realized, to keep them from merely stuffing themselves and chatting, but what? It was his funeral. He should be in the limelight.

Hiding his irritation, he returned to his seat. The people had dispersed. As a result, the coffin loomed larger. He lit another cigarette. What should he do?

And at that very minute, as he was about to give up, what appeared out of nowhere was the plaster cast he had worn as a child to fix his broken arm. Ghostly white at first, as white as the coffin, it had been covered, at school, with scribbles long before lunch was served. Everyone had joined in. There had been no felt-tip pens in those days, but there were Biros, most with blue ink, a few with black or red. "Get well," one of his classmates had written – tags and graffiti had not yet become commonplace, though some daredevil might scratch his name into a desktop. "Get better," the class comedian countered. There had been rhymes, one or two lines, from a couple of girls, and a heart, in rough outline, from one, pierced by an arrow. "Forever." What was her name? Viviane? And inevitably, since he had been a sitting duck, there had been an "Eff off" scrawled just out of reach, which his mother had effaced with an emery board.

Yes, he had concluded, elated, it could be done. Not with Biros, maybe, but with felt pens. Different-sized tips. Permanent ink. Acrylic paints for those with an artistic bent.

The coffin transformed into a giant guest book, no less.

Hawkins had reconsidered the set-up.

Instead of the customary procession of people advancing in small groups, in order of rank as determined by the closeness of their relationship with the deceased, stopping momentarily around the coffin with their heads down, a flower or two at the ready; instead of that, there would be creative chaos. They could write or sketch anything: a greeting, a thank-you note, a brief recollection. Children, who love to draw on walls, could decorate the sides, grown-ups the lid. There should be enough space for everyone – if not, the result would form an intriguing palimpsest, which would be equally appropriate.

And he would be there, the focus of everything that transpired.

"William, we love you!"

He had gone to tell Debra.

"And that's it?"

She had been in the kitchen, on the phone. It was coming up to dinnertime, but there was no smell of cooking; there never is. She orders takeaways. "It's either that or we eat out," she had established early in their relationship and he had assumed she would come to her senses, sooner or later. He had been wrong.

52

"What do you mean?"

Her glance had bounced off him. "A sort of happening?"

"I suppose."

"Without a script? And no elegies? No…" A moment's hesitation. "No MC?"

She is more familiar with DJs than MCs. Well, one is the popular version of the other.

He had corrected her: "Eulogies." But she had a point. They would want instructions, encouragement. They couldn't simply be left to their own devices. "That's what the rehearsal's for," he had reminded her. "I'll walk them through it."

"I thought you were going to play dead."

Was that a seductive smile? Not very long ago he had known instinctively. He had tried to mirror it. "Not that dead."

But she was done with the subject. "Have it your way." And she had floated past him in unconcern.

The coffin had been granted a temporary home in the box room, paint, brushes and pens secreted inside. Thus unencumbered, Hawkins had given some consideration not only to the guest list, a problematic issue in view of his strained relations with his family, but also to his obituary. Formally, he was aware, the latter would have to be presented as someone else's work, but as with company reports, he was the one closest to the facts, best able to angle them in the interest of… well, in the final analysis, he had to allow, of himself. The audience, of course, differed; no longer addressing shareholders or future investors, he hoped, all the same, that his example might inspire others to put their best foot forward, and was pleased with what he accomplished as his own ghostwriter, in spite of the unusual format – using "he" and not "we" was something of a stumbling block. A little close to a letter of application, the draft yet made his heart beat faster. Needless to say, whoever came to lend his name to the final text would want to add an anecdote or two, but that would do no harm. Avoiding what might strike the reader as boasts, he had clamped down on the personal.

Selecting who to invite had proved a lot tougher. Leaving out family initially, he had quickly jotted down the names of some obvious choices: an MP, a local councillor, three board members – from different fields, to avoid shoptalk. Having got that far, he had broken off. What if everything went wrong? Could he face these people professionally if his plans failed? What if Crawley heard of it? The word would spread like wildfire. He crossed them out.

Who could he safely ask?

His mind had gone completely blank.

"Debra," he had said that night at dinner, adopting a casual tone, "who shall we invite to the 'happening'?" He poked at the sushi she had ordered. Whatever happened to plain fish and chips?

"Huh?"

She had forgotten.

"The rehearsal. My funeral."

"Oh, that." She licked her fingers.

Still sensuous, he had decided.

She took a drink. "Who would you want?"

"As many as possible of those who will be there eventually."

She had examined something green that for him had no name, let it tickle her lips. "I doubt that my people would show up."

"For my funeral?" He had laid down his fork.

54

"That they might. I meant for your practice do."

This called for diplomacy. "What if we don't tell them?"

"In that case they definitely wouldn't. How could they?" She had tilted her head, her eyes opened wide.

He had waited for the sigh that should accompany the expression.

It came.

"I mean, if we don't let on why. We just invite them to… to…" How convince her? "To a soiree?"

"Is that a happening?"

"It could be." He had smiled. Her innocence remains her chief asset. "It means some form of evening entertainment. A performance, involving music, perhaps. Dance. Ballet. Nothing pretentious. It would fit what I have in mind."

"They would like that."

So soiree was the name they had given it. They had agreed on a date, hired a caterer for a buffet meal. Written invitations had gone out, without an RSVP, to minimize the risk of contact and a negative response. Once the guests crossed the threshold, they couldn't very well turn tail. Her relatives would be there in full force. On his side, his hope stood to three cousins, a handful of minor business associates who would feel honoured that they had been included, and his sons. His ex-wives were a must but would most likely tear up the invitation post-haste. "Your presence will make a world of difference," he had written at the bottom of the cards for Lester and for Todd and his wife. Be there, he had wanted to add, but what kind of threat would be effective? Could sons be disinherited in this day and age? And if they could, would that persuade them? He had thought not.

They had arranged to have most of the furniture

removed, the coffin placed on a stand, centrally, on the day of the event.

"Couldn't we leave it in the library?" Debra had been her most seductive. "It will be such a dampener."

"Not if we do this right." With a flourish, he would raise the lid and produce the tubes of acrylic paint, brushes, sets of felt pens he had stored away. "I'm sure they'll enjoy themselves. As long as enough of them turn up, there shouldn't be a problem."

He had laid an arm around her, imagining the coffin nicely lit up. There had been no response. She had withdrawn into a world of her own, to which he had no access.

And now it is here, the day he has been waiting for, worried about – why else the nightmare? Not having the use of his car, which is locked in the garage, he gets home a little later than intended. The furniture is in the drive, as agreed – their neighbours will be wondering what is up. He walks quickly past the drawing room, catching a glimpse of the buffet and a corner of the coffin. There are spotlights here and there – a nice touch. Debra is a dab hand at arranging parties. A quick shower and a change and he will be ready.

It is as he is drying himself that he hears a deep bass sound from downstairs – the shower must have drowned it out. He opens the door a fraction; Debra, he concludes, has put on some music while waiting. Is she also tense? The beat travels through the woodwork. She will have to switch it off before their guests arrive.

But Debra is only indirectly behind the music. "This is Homespun," she announces, as Hawkins enters the room; she gestures towards a man of her own age, wearing a T-shirt that indeed proclaims that Homespun is his name. He stands beside a table full of gadgets that, except for a headset – two headsets – turntables and a microphone, Hawkins is unable to identify. There is a nest of cables.

"Hawkins." If he appears brusque, so be it. "What's the meaning of this?"

Debra's face is aglow. "The entertainment, darling. I kept it a secret to surprise you. Aren't you pleased?"

Homespun joins in. "When Debs here first got in touch, I considered ambient. But you'd mentioned dancing, she said, and with a mixed age group, house will go down better; that is, house merged with drum 'n' bass. A bit of house, a bit of drum 'n' bass. That'll get people going."

Ambient. House. Drum 'n' bass. Fashions come and go; to Hawkins, they all spell disco. The man is a DJ.

"This is a funeral."

"My first." Homespun breaks into a smile. "It's a great idea. I've done mainly weddings and parties. Debs suggested I make a clip and post it on YouTube. You'll be setting a trend."

"But…" Now it is Hawkins who makes a gesture, meant to direct their attention to the coffin. But the coffin isn't there; it has been relocated to the far corner, set at an angle in order to leave more floor space. The lights point at the DJ's stand.

"It's temporary." Debra studies his face. "During the soiree part. People will love it."

Hawkins wonders if she means the dancing or the coffin, but that is immaterial. Were he to put his foot down, those on her side of the guest list would get wind of it and walk out. He can't have that.

"What's your field, Mr. Hawkins?" Homespun beams.

"Transportation."

"That figures. Well, if everything works out, your friends should be transported tonight." He makes a thumbs-up sign and returns to his equipment.

He has the right attitude, Hawkins will give him that. But a disco?

Regardless of his misgivings, the doorbell forestalls any rearrangement. And as soon as the first guests have made an entrance, others follow – it is as if they had been waiting outside for there to be a sufficient number to face the ordeal. The room starts filling up, the way he had imagined it. Presently Homespun has his equipment going and though there is no dancing as such, an arm, a knee, moves with the music. Two girls who must be from the catering firm help out at the buffet; a man is in charge of the drinks. Hawkins shakes a hand here and there, pats someone's shoulder, picks up snatches of conversation. Not surprisingly, perhaps, people shy away from the coffin – the reason they have been invited.

"What's it doing here?" Debra's sister asks her boyfriend as Hawkins passes by.

"Beats me," the boy replies.

"A carpe diem," someone offers.

"Uh?" But the girl doesn't really want an answer; she heads for the buffet, where she feels at home. "Ah! Thai food! Oh, this is great. Let's enjoy ourselves!"

And they seem to. But Hawkins notes each time the doorbell rings that, apart from a cousin and an obsequious colleague – one out of the five he had invited – they are Debra's people. In part, this is natural: given the difference in age, his circle has dwindled compared to hers – his family tree has been cropped. But not hinting at the nature of the event may have been unwise. He could have used separate cards for Debra's kith and kin. The reference to a soiree would bring – had brought – them. It might have intrigued Alison and Barbara but had not provided sufficient bait for them to rise above their disinclination to join him for an evening. And Lester and Todd? He couldn't

58

even hazard a guess. The few words he had scrawled on theirs may not have won them over. No doubt they still hold his divorce from their mother against him, in spite of the overly generous settlement her lawyer got her.

Homespun's music cuts into his musings. Phrases repeat themselves: "Keep listening... Keep listening... Keep listening... Keep listening..." "Don't make me... Don't make me... Don't... Don't... Don't..." The words go nowhere. Along with the bass and the drums they form a treadmill for the dancers – for now, some are actually dancing – who, undeterred by the volume, carry on shouted conversations. Maybe they regard the sound level as a challenge that has to be met.

For him it is his sons that constitute the challenge.

What he should do, of course, is phone them. Hawkins nods and happens to catch Debra's eye. She smiles, bobbing her head in apparent agreement. Truly, what harm can it do? Half an hour, he reckons; he will give them half an hour and she seconds that into the bargain before twirling around towards Homespun's table, her arms shaking alongside those of her partner.

But why prolong the agony? If they are on their way, fine. If not, the sooner he gets hold of them, the better.

He takes himself outside and settles into one of the chairs in the drive, his back to the house. His thumb finds Todd's number – his PA dug it up after the birth of the twins. That had been his last attempt to contact either of them. He lets the phone ring, but there is no reply. Will the display reveal who called or merely the number?

He lights a cigarette for a renewed effort. The voice that finally breaks the silence could be anyone's.

"What do you want?"

Startled by its abruptness, Hawkins stumbles over the words: "It's... I'm... That is, we're..." Taking a deep breath, he collects himself. "Listen Todd, I sent you an invitation." And he explains what is afoot.

But Todd cuts him short.

"There's nothing I could think of that would bring me to your funeral."

"But I'm your father!"

A stray dog sniffs at one of the tables, lifts its leg. Hawkins gets up, but it is too late. The dog wanders off, nose to the ground.

"Not much of one."

"I couldn't always be there." He sits down.

"Even if you were."

"I had my work…" Hawkins stops. "What do you mean?"

"You had your work."

"Yes." What is the boy suggesting? "Anyway…"

Once more he is interrupted.

"Remember that winter you took me skiing?"

The dog is back. Hawkins gets up.

"Hold on a second." He puts the phone down, sets off towards the animal. Defiantly, it seems, it raises its leg in the very same spot, taking good aim. Hawkins's foot misses its target.

"Sorry about that. Are you there?"

"Yes." Todd is clearly nettled. "Unlike you."

"I said I was sorry. So, I took you skiing…? What's that got to do with anything?"

"It shows how things stood between us. I must have been seven or eight. Remember? A family weekend? Up north? Our only one? Except Lester was staying with a friend."

Hawkins pulls on his cigarette. "I don't, but never mind. Tell me."

"It was my first time on skis."

60

"Well, if you were eight that's not surprising. What happened?"

"It was like in that fable. The tortoise and the hare. You must have read it."

"A fable? No."

"They had a race. And the hare was faster, naturally, but lay down here and there for a nap. Then the tortoise caught up. You were the hare; I was the tortoise. You stopped as well, but the minute I was within sight of you, you disappeared. Again and again. In the fable, the tortoise won. For me, the outcome was different. When I finally got there, you had already handed in your skis and were waiting by the car."

Hawkins considers what Todd has told him. If it did happen, it has left no trace. "Well, it taught you not to give up, didn't it?"

He hears a sigh.

"Didn't it?"

But Todd sounds sceptical. "If anything, it taught me that you view life as a contest. For you, the one thing that matters is to come out on top. But that probably didn't strike me until later."

"It's not a bad philosophy."

"I think it is."

"Well, we differ." They are at a standstill. Obviously Todd won't listen. Hawkins dismisses him and changes tack. "Can you give me Lester's number?"

The answer is immediate. "No."

"No?" He must have it, surely, or have the brothers fallen out?

There is a brief silence. Todd's response, after that pause, includes no apologies. "He doesn't want me to pass it on."

Hawkins drops his cigarette between his feet and kills it. "To me, or generally?"

"To you."

"And did he let on why?"

"He didn't have to. I knew how he felt about you. Because of what you did to Mum. And to him, evidently."

"To him?" The line is silent. "Are you there?"

"To him," Todd repeats.

The dog has returned. Hawkins ignores it.

"I have no idea what you're referring to."

"Well, I can't enlighten you. He won't go into specifics."

Hawkins racks his memory but nothing offers itself. Has the boy gone nutty?

As if in reply, Todd adds: "He's been seeing a shrink for the last two years."

"Pshaw!"

The phone slips out of his hand. Once he has retrieved it, the line is dead. He checks the display. Should he persist? But what purpose would it serve? Either Todd is having him on or else Lester has gone off his head. Neither of them will put in an appearance, that much is clear, not tonight, nor at the actual funeral. He makes a sudden dash towards the dog but stumbles. It gets away.

Damn.

Inside, two cigarettes later, the music is maintaining the same insistent beat, with no marked transition between tracks. All overlap. There are no pauses. There is no discernible tune. There are no lyrics as such. Unaffected by the rhythm, by the bustle around him, Hawkins crosses the room, manoeuvring between couples, threesomes, foursomes, heading for the improvised bar. He points towards a bottle and then, having picked up his glass, walks over to the coffin. In the absence of tables, he places the glass on the lid, off-white in the semi-darkness. He swears under his breath. This isn't going his way. Is he to lie there one day, boxed in, with no one but Debra's folk paying their respects? If that is the word for it – a DJ playing drum 'n' bass. He should get into it this minute, push the pots of paint, the brushes and the pens aside and pull the lid up over him. It is as if he weren't there.

Staring at a knot near one of the handles, he senses Crawley's leer as the man scratches an obscenity into the wood.

He tastes the wine. Whiskey would have been better.

"Who's in it?"

The voice belongs to a stranger. Well, he is as welcome there as any of them. Hawkins shrugs. At least the man is evincing an interest in what should be the principal focus of everyone.

"No one as yet."

"But at the end of the day…"

"… we'll all find ourselves in one."

The kayak, he reflects. He should have picked the kayak. If he had, and if they hadn't disowned him, Lester and Todd could have set fire to it and pushed it out to sea – a Viking warrior, sword at his side, a shield covering his chest, a horned helmet completing the outfit, leaving for Valhalla, aflame. That would have been something. There would have been no call for any other props or decorations – or for words. The act would speak for itself.

The stranger is gone. Hawkins watches him saunter over to the buffet, hand one of the girls his plate and head for the door. That is what the others should be doing too. None of those present fit his plans. What could they scribble on the coffin that would have any bearing on the life he has led? What could their contribution be other than clichés? *You'll be in our hearts always.* Oh yeah? The kids at school had demonstrated greater ingenuity.

Keep it up, he prompts the crowd. Eat, drink and be merry! There will be no mock funeral tonight. Perhaps not ever.

Having emptied his glass, he scans the room until he catches sight of Debra. If she is the least bit tired, there are no signs of it. With her arms bent at the elbow, her head and shoulders shake to the beat. This is her life. For a fleeting moment she becomes Alison when Alison was her age and whispered to him, at one of their parties, that she was carrying his child. Lester. The music is different, but their movements much the same. He had watched Alison that night with similar intensity. Pregnant. He blinks and Debra is back. He shuts his eyes. What if...? For years, sons, family, have meant Lester and Todd to the exclusion of anything else, but that needn't be the case. Why shouldn't Debra, like Alison, give him a child? He would make it pay off. A son, brought up to stand by his father, to show respect, to follow, in contrast to Lester and Todd, in his footsteps. What is to say it cannot be? As the idea takes hold, he is captured by the music. His hips join Debra's, a little offbeat, and there he is, performing a slow dance at the head of the coffin. Hesitant at first, not altogether sure of himself, but dancing as he has rarely danced in the past, he begins to cross the room. People clear a path for him, alerted to his goal and undeniably expressing their approval. Be with me, he implores his wife; be with me and everything will be well.

Coming up from behind, he places his hands gently on her shoulders, his lips brushing her neck.

"Mrs. Hawkins?"

She moves with him, within his embrace, until she faces him.

"I don't know where I would be without you."

She smiles her appreciation. Her hips are in sync with his.

"I'll put the funeral on hold."

Another smile. The others retreat a fraction, forming a circle. There is a slow handclap, building in volume. The years stretch ahead of him, full of promise. He will age with his coffin.

A son.

A son, to give him the right send-off.

As if in support, Homespun's disc repeats the phrase he had caught earlier: "Keep listening… Keep listening…"

That is good advice.

A little awkwardly he sways this way and that, then gyrates while the clapping increases both in speed and volume, reaching a crescendo. Everyone is on his side.

He will tell her tonight.

Oh! she will cry. *Oh! Oh, William!*

A son.

Tonight.

Tonight.

He'll send for the kayak in the morning.

The Race

His past caught up with him just before dawn. It seemed so unfair: the odds had definitely been on his side. Crouching, his feet pushing against the blocks, he'd got off to a good start. He'd gained the inner lane. Nothing had weighed him down. Then slowly, unaccountably, he'd heard it closing in. He'd felt its breath as it transferred its burden, one piece at a time, easing its load, adding to his. He'd stumbled, fallen – till finally, bereft of all hope for the future, he hid under the bed.

At age fifteen!

Episode

There is no beginning. I am simply there, looking at the
man beside the taxi. It is no one I recognize. The back door
is open. Another man is lying on the seat, his feet sticking
out. That is my father.

The stranger's voice is slurred.

"You take his legs."

I hesitate. "What's wrong with him?"

"You could say he's had one too many."

"You from his office?"

"Nah. His lodge."

I don't know what a lodge is.

"He'll tell you. How old are you?"

"Eleven."

"Will you manage? Your mother looked stronger."

I shrug. "I'll manage."

I do, but I have to rest on each landing.

And that is it. Not only is there no beginning – there is
no ending either. It is as if I had abandoned my father on
the top landing, outside the flat where we lived, forever
excluded, no longer part of my life.

Now, years later, I can supply some of what is missing.
Although it left no imprint, my father must have been home
to dress for the event, his first appearance, perhaps the only
one, at some lodge, which in all likelihood took the form of
an initiation ceremony. By bedtime, that is, my bedtime, he
was probably already nearing the limit of what he could
take. Another glass or two of whatever he was having
would have put him out. He wasn't that much of a drinker.

But the lack of a proper beginning bothers me. The man
who brought my father home must have come to the door –
how else would he have known that my mother looked
stronger than me? What had he said? *Your husband's*

outside in a cab. He's out cold. You'll have to give me a hand. Would that have been it? And what had been her reaction? Had she been angry? Upset? Disgusted? I just don't know. Neither the next day nor at some later point did she so much as allude to the incident. The fact that she didn't go down herself but sent me suggests that she wanted to have nothing to do with it. Nor can I recall what words she used when she came to wake me. They would have constituted a command and not a plea, of that I am sure: *You have to get dressed. Your father needs help* – the reference would be to "Your father" even at that point, not Dad or Daddy. But this is pure speculation. You would expect something so out of the ordinary to remain imprinted on my mind in all its details, but there is nothing there except the taxi and the slow climb up the stairs.

My father didn't talk about it either. For all I know, he may never have learned who carried him upstairs.

The two of them must have talked, though, husband and wife. My father must have come to with few if any recollections of the night before, presumably still fully dressed unless my mother had taken care to remove his shoes. He would have looked around, confused, the sharp light hurting his eyes, his head pounding, and found himself, where? On the living-room couch? In their bedroom? My mother would have been nowhere around. He would have got up awkwardly and gone to look for her. And there I have to end all speculation: what took place between them is part of a story I didn't get to hear. In fact, all of that morning is a blank. In the months that followed, my father slept in the living room as often as not; the explanation that I didn't ask for was that the bedroom was too warm. But that first morning left no echo in my mind of angry voices, nor the oppressive weight of suffocating silences. There is nothing.

68

There is nothing until late in the afternoon. "Would you two like to go to the cinema?" my mother asked. "Would you, Geoffrey? Peter?" Of course we would, my brother and I. "Right," she said. "Tell your father I'm taking you." When I realized he was to be excluded, I hesitated, momentarily, but Peter, for whom this would be the first time ever, shouted: "Daddy! Mummy's taking us to the pictures!" without any attempt from her to stop him from yelling, as she would have done in normal circumstances.

Pictures for punishment. The treat that only I had experienced until that day, reserved for special occasions, had been changed into its opposite, not for me but for my father, the one who had taken me the few times I had been, while Peter, five years younger, had had to stay at home. There weren't many films suitable for both of us.

Star Wars was, my mother had decided. She read the title and the brief introduction aloud for Peter's benefit as the film started; I pointed out that the number was wrong: it should be *Episode I*, not *IV*. Eleven-year-olds are such know-it-alls. Now, at forty-eight, I can account for the numbering of the *Star Wars* sequence, but I am less sure of myself in other areas. For one thing, memory, I have learned, tends to play tricks on you.

Mostly, of course, what happens leaves no trace at all: so little is retained. That is the case with the first few years of my life; I recall hardly anything until I was five. That must be when the photo was taken – the photo that came in the post and brought to mind, again, the night and the afternoon I would as soon forget; the man, the taxi, the trudge up the stairs; the bitter treat. The photo itself holds no memories. It is one I haven't seen before. It is of a scene that I don't recognize. In it, my father is sitting on the ground, leaning against a wall; I am standing beside him. We are both squinting into the sun. The shadow cast by the photographer reaches my father's feet. I assume it is my mother's, but there is no telling; the compressed dark shape has no traits by which it can be identified. There is no Peter. "Thought you might want this," says the note that was enclosed with it. "Your Dad."

If the picture was to have a caption, it should read "Father and son", I decide. Or maybe not – why state the obvious? "At the seaside" would be a better choice. There is no sea, but the wall, whitewashed, rough, is of the type that separates roads or car parks from the beach in many places. I am wearing shorts and a T-shirt, my father, always the businessman, plain grey trousers and a light blue and white striped shirt, the button-down collar and the absence of jacket and tie his only concession to the setting. Neither of us will go swimming, I am certain, though the season may be right.

Are we happy? It is hard to tell. The photo is as sharp as can be expected of one taken, presumably, with a cheap camera, but there are necessarily few details: it is the standard size print produced by the shops in those days. If neither of us is laughing, nor do we look sad. We are close but not touching. The scene has a generic quality: there is nothing to suggest that the same photo couldn't be taken again and again for many years to come, father and son together, symbolically protected by the wall behind us from anything that might pose a threat.

That hadn't come to be. It couldn't, needless to say: nothing lasts. What remains in this instance are a few words and the photograph: "Thought you might want this." Unreasonably, that is precisely what I want, for even though I don't remember the event, I do indeed want to be five, I want my father to be there beside me, leaning against the wall, I want to squint into the sun and see my mother and the camera and hear the shutter click and have her walk towards us and my father take her place so she can sit beside me in her turn, or better still, ask some passing stranger to please take a picture of the three of us together and so freeze the moment and not let time move on and have us go, inevitably, each our separate way.

Just how that separation came about I am unable to say. For a long time I blamed my father. I blamed my mother. Later I blamed myself, mostly for shutting my father out, both shamefully and shamelessly, after the night I helped to carry him upstairs, making of that a divider that it may not have been. Confused, I stayed out much of the time, teaming up with an older boy from another school, to play football, the two of us, taking turns as goalkeeper, or to spy on girls, or to make our way onto forbidden building sites, where we would fantasize about running away with a travelling circus. When my father walked out, one month and three days before my twelfth birthday, I wasn't even home.

I take down the photo album from the bookcase, an unfinished project begun long ago, and open it, uncertain of how far I got – most of the pictures that haven't been thrown away or lost are in folders in my desk, along with strips of negatives. The album starts, I see, not the way I thought with studio shots of my parents, but with me as a baby – photos that I may have found interesting until age six or seven but probably not after that. Next comes my first birthday, followed by outdoor scenes interrupted by birthdays two, and three, and four: there I am, on my feet, standing or walking or sitting on a swing or in a sandpit, demolishing a sandcastle, built no doubt by someone else, with a small plastic spade, or tripping over a football, with a look of surprise. In the last picture, at the top of a page, I am in the garden of a house I recognize as ours, before we moved. There was, I know, a fence and a gate that I was not to open, leading onto a park or village green. If the pictures come in the right order, I would have been four at the time – the pictures of my fifth birthday, if there are any, must be in the desk.

A memory surfaces abruptly: I hear loud voices from a crowd of people in the park beyond the fence and close my eyes to try and recall the scene. This I can't do with any certainty. The people are excited. Are they laughing? They may be. I must have looked up at the kitchen window and, seeing no one there, squeezed through the gate, but this is no more than a guess. The crowd forms a dense wall. Suddenly a gap opens up and through the gap I see a man on the ground, screaming, staring at some ghastly sight above him, kicking his legs, flailing his arms. It is scary. The gap closes. I back away.

The incident is no less confusing now than it must have been when it occurred, which may be why it has stayed with me all these years, however incomplete, to reappear at a time when so much else is gone. "Just some drunk," I hear my mother say. "Let's see what's on TV" – or was that on a different occasion altogether? I couldn't say.

"Just some drunk." I close the album, snap it shut: it has a strap and a small buckle, as if to keep the photos safely locked away. Someday I must finish the project and add whatever pictures I would like to keep. I should at least move past my childhood, into my teens – my fatherless years. But that is not an accurate description of what followed: I am as fatherless today as I was then.

Still, nothing can change that. The note, the only one I have received in over thirty years, has it right, except for the tense: "Thought you might want this." Would have wanted, it should have said – and not just the photo, then. I put it back in the envelope. Too bad it never came to be.

Cat in the Snow

There was the miscarriage; there was the cat. She connected the two. Who wouldn't? But very soon doubt entered her mind. Was life ever that simple? If it was, why at this point? Why not the first time around? And why a cat? In some ways she shared Robert's opinion. "Dogs," he had said on one occasion, eyeing a Rottweiler that was charging down the street, a broken chain clattering behind it. "Dogs are useful." A hair's breadth ahead a cat squeezed under a fence. Phew! Dee shivered at the memory. "They'll fetch and carry. They'll protect you. They'll die for you. A cat will only save its own skin. What good is that?" Now, she wouldn't stand by to see a cat butchered by a Rottweiler, but other than that she agreed. Cats were no more special than, say, crickets.

So when she first caught sight of it out back, beside the small greenhouse, she noted its presence but that was all. Even that took some doing: she could barely make out the shape in the snow, not primarily because of its spectral whiteness, but because it kept so still. It took an effort to trace the opaque eyes, which neither blinked nor shifted position, and the pale pink nose, held rigidly still. She had no idea what possessed her to crouch down, once she was convinced those were eyes, that was a nose, and call out, but no matter: the cat didn't respond. To Dee, that was a mark of past abuse, if not from Rottweilers then from some human beast. Perhaps to make up for it she got a small bowl and a couple of tins of cat food from the pet shop the same afternoon. She placed the bowl in the spot where the cat had been and lingered for a while. The cat had left no imprint in the snow.

Inside Robert's voice greeted her.

"Did you go out at all today?"

"Briefly," she told him.

"You know what the doctor recommended."

"I know," she said. "Well, it was less than that."

"Why don't you try swimming?"

But she shook her head. She didn't feel at home in her body just yet. She wasn't sure how far she could trust it.

The food was still there in the morning. She picked up the bowl. "Here, cat," she called, rattling the frozen bits in case the cat was within hearing. A name would simplify things. Kitty? Molly? Snowy? Of course, whatever common name she chose might well be tainted. The gender posed another problem. Should it be male or female or, given the times, both? Female, probably, since the cat appeared to have been abused. Dee played with variations of her own name. Audrey? Deirdre? Delia? She tested them one at a time. Both whispered and spoken aloud she found the sound of Delia the most appealing. The movement of her tongue was pleasingly smooth, as it shifted gently from the ridge behind her upper teeth to the area a little further back before lowering itself to let the final vowel through. *De-li-a.* Spoken too fast, it became a sloppy *De-l-ya.* No cat would want that. "De-li-a," she called. "Here, De-li-a." No shadow moved across the snow.

To occupy herself she carefully inscribed the name on the side of the bowl, pausing after each stroke, worried that the marker would slip on the glossy surface. She didn't dare try curlicues and so the result was a lot less smooth than she would have liked it, especially when it came to the three rounded letters: they wound up much too angular. Worse, all five of them seemed bristly. She had used permanent black ink, but turpentine might remove it all the same. Would a renewed effort pay off? She thought not. She refilled the bowl and put it back outside. She would wait for the cat's reaction.

But reaction there was none, if you didn't regard the disappearance of the food as one. By late afternoon every last scrap was gone. The name had not put the cat off, nor had the smell of ink. Bending down to bring the bowl inside, Dee saw a bird hiding in the bushes and shooed it away. "It's cat food," she said. She immediately regretted the action. What if the cat had left a morsel as bait, preferring wild game to factory food, and had been ready to spring on the bird the moment Dee opened the door? She glanced at the empty bowl. Birdseed was the answer. She could make another trip to the shop. She tried to imagine a brief exchange with Robert on the topic. "Today I went for a walk," she could say. "I was clean out of bird food." But she was unable to think of a reply. There were so many things they'd never talked about, bird food being just one. They'd never had any, had they? But the bird would hardly come back in a hurry – it would be dark shortly. In any case, the cat may very well have eaten all the food herself, not caring in the least for birds. Dee pictured her with a limp bird in her claws and saw her gag on blood-stained down and bits of bone. She erased the image. That wasn't the sort of cat she'd want in her garden.

Over the next few days, she filled the bowl morning and night, as if the initial feed had made the cat her responsibility. It called for persistence: she hadn't seen the animal after that first time, even though she'd been getting up earlier than she used to, before it was properly light – cats hunted at dawn and dusk, didn't they? Having the bedroom to herself helped. That only used to happen when Robert was away at a conference or for a job interview. Mostly he'd let her know both when and where, and maybe even why, but at times it had slipped his mind. Or hers? On those occasions she had always worried, unable to appreciate the space his absence afforded her. Now she no longer had that worry.

Delia had found a space for herself too, Dee discovered late one day, but again she had to look twice to be quite sure she wasn't seeing things. Legs tucked in under her, the cat was one almost with the white bonnet of her neighbour's car where it stood in the driveway, the engine presumably giving off heat after a recent run. In the low sunlight, it was the translucent blue of her eyes that gave the cat away. "You'd be better off on my side of the hedge," Dee warned her. Judging from what little she had seen of people in the area, they weren't likely to throw their doors open to strangers, let alone cats. Her neighbour's leaf blower would make short work of her. Not that Dee differed greatly in terms of hospitality; she wouldn't want a cat in the house herself. They marked their territory, indoors and out. They made scratch marks. They tore things. A life without a cat suited her fine.

But what good was her resolve? She had no sooner confirmed it when the cat made her way in.

"How was your day?" she heard Robert ask.

"No different," she told him.

"You have to eat. The doc—"

"I know." She shouldn't cut him short. "I will," she said, out of habit, to oblige, as if it would make the least difference. Why be so solicitous? "It was none of my doing," he had insisted. "You brought it on yourself." She went into the kitchen and opened the door to the fridge. There were eggs. She didn't want eggs. There were sausages. How long had she had those? They would be off, wouldn't they? There was very little else. She disposed of the sausages and made herself a cheese omelette. Then, frying pan in hand, she turned around and there, perched on the shelf that held her two cookery books and the tea caddy, was the cat. She returned the pan to the cooker with a clank and spun around to face her – but too late. The cat was gone, having left not even a draught behind. The cookery books stood undisturbed the way they had for months. The metal tea caddy bore no smudge mark that could be attributed to a cat's nose. Dee stared in disbelief.

"Eat," she told herself. She transferred the omelette to her plate and moved the plate so she would face the doorway rather than the window. "Eat. Then search all the rooms."

She did, but saw no sign of a cat – she even crossed the threshold of what had again become the spare room, a space she knew not how to fill. How had it got in? And, more to the point, where had it gone? Had she forgotten to pull the door to? Had it slunk in alongside her? Had someone let it in? Robert? Had he, without her knowledge, had a new key made? Having nothing but questions she inspected the ground-floor windows one more time, but everything was as it should be.

To ease the tension that had built up, she made herself a cup of tea and took it into the sitting room, where her chair welcomed her back. Weeks must have passed. The cramps. The bleeding. The uncertainty. Here, too, across the room, were shelves, half emptied out, which could have held a whole litter of cats – she had read of old women whose cats came to fill the entire house. Out of the corner of her eye she caught sight of a small urn, a wedding gift she hadn't seen for years. Had it not shattered? She couldn't recall mending it. She blinked and it was gone. Once spring arrived she would pick vases of flowers to bring the room to life.

She closed her eyes. Before her was a path deep in the woods, with sunlight filtering through light green leaves, a carpet of wood anemones – cowslips would come later, wouldn't they? – and butterflies dancing in the air. Violets? A cat – Delia – was coming towards her, with two, no three kittens in tow, one black, one white, one tiger striped, sniffing the flowers, swiping at the butterflies. There must have been a father, but he was gone, missed by no one. Why should they care? Delia would do for them.

Dee opened her eyes to blot out the picture and heard Delia hiss.

She would have been smaller even than those kittens not so long ago.

"I could have done for you," she said.

But why waste sentiment on a cat that came and went as it pleased?

Still, conscientiously, she put out food morning and night and Delia, equally conscientiously, licked the bowl clean. At one time winter loosened its grip for a few days and Dee left the door ajar, to air the house. But air was all that entered. From inside she perceived a dull thud as snow slid off the roof. Another followed. She stepped out to size up the mounds, checking that there was no overhang above the door. Some of her neighbours' roofs were much steeper than hers. Could they prove hazardous to the cat? They might, she decided, if there were icicles as well as snow. But what could she do? The cat just had to take its chances. Rottweilers. Leaf blowers. Ice. That the food disappeared proved that she was as yet unharmed.

Then one day winter was truly on the wane. The sun rose earlier and as Dee placed her breakfast cup on the arm of her chair in the sitting room, its rays played on the wall across from her. "Here, pet," she whispered, and there was the cat on one of the shelves, her coat electrified. Dee caressed her with her eyes, exulting in her perfect shape, her colouring, her poise, noting the exquisite grace with which each action was performed, her ears turning almost imperceptibly at the least sound, the pink inside changing in aspect as the light hit it at a different angle, her whiskers floating on the air in perfect symmetry, the muscles of her body playing as she stretched, pushing her front paws out, pulling them in, her tail one moment a sorcerer's wand, the next a bullwhip. However slight the variations were,

78

Dee was transfixed. She could have watched the cat all day.

"My Delia," she said. She was aware of a faint miaow in reply and reached out. But there was no one there.

No one there. No one anywhere.

She closed her eyes but doing so shut nothing out, brought nothing into view.

That night she went to bed without having gone near the back garden. Let the cat fend for itself, she decided. Let it catch birds – there were more of them each day. Who cares if it chokes on the feathers? Let it live off what nature has to offer. Let it try its luck with the neighbours.

She slept badly, hearing the cat in her sleep. Near dawn she all but gave up: the cat, she felt, was in the bedroom with her, moving about restlessly. She examined the top of the wardrobe, the dresser, the space under the chair that was in part covered by her clothes, but saw not a trace of her. Again she tried to bring on sleep, taking slow breaths, but sleep wouldn't come. Finally, in the early morning, she must have dozed off.

What woke her was the cat's slow progress from the foot end of the bed, each movement so minimal that it assured her she was dreaming. It crept along her legs. Gently she drew back the cover to make room for it beside her; it curled up on her stomach and started purring. Warmth spread through her like an infusion of new blood. Their breathing synchronized. There was no outside world.

And then the outside world intruded, as Dee sought the softness of Delia's coat. What her hand came to rest on was no cat. There were no pointed ears, no whiskers, no tail. What her fingers caressed wasn't fur but skin, cold to the touch. "No," she whispered. A shiver ran through her. "Don't. Please don't. I never wanted you. I never did." Her words hung in the air. But the claim, no more true than the reverse, brought only pain.

Scene: Another Part of the Island

I shouldn't have slowed down, but then, how could I not? The phrase she used hooked me; the vintage hat and suit, the handbag pinned to her side reeled me in. "I'm an inebriated person," she said, negotiating the syllables one at a time. I'd had one or two whiskies myself and was in a mellow mood; once I knew the direction, I was happy to help her over each obstacle, doing a lip-synch: *I-ne-bri-a-ted.* "That's why I'm keeping still. Dogs can sense it." One of her feet left her at that point; she brought it back successfully. Tipsy or any of the standard culinary choices – soaked, pickled, stewed – would have accomplished nothing. Inebriated coupled with person was what did it. I smiled.

"Mine's been around," I assured her.

Like me, he had spotted her from afar. Her right hand, given free play for balance, had persuaded him there was a dog attached to the end of the invisible lead. Who else but someone walking a dog would have business in the park at night? He had strained. He had sniffed the air. Now, disappointed, he raised his leg to mark the lamppost where she stood.

"Been around what?" she asked. She hit me coquettishly with the handbag, using more force perhaps than she was quite aware, given her state. She was a big woman, her height, if not her weight, nearly matching mine. Then she became serious. She lectured me. "Dogs never forget. If anybody with even a trace of alcohol on their breath ever hurt them, and all it takes is a thimbleful, they remember. One whiff and they go for you." She glanced at Caliban. I instantly shortened both his lead and his name.

"Cal wouldn't."

The day had been close. A distant rumble followed my words, as if to back them up.

"Of course," she added, oblivious to the sound, "not being around can also cause trauma."

She looked at me, making the statement personal. I hesitated, but decided to take no notice. I'm no father confessor.

"I don't doubt it," I said.

"Being left out. Ignored. Deserted."

I nodded. She had reeled me in; she was getting the net ready. "He is not the least bit aggressive," I insisted. Caliban, a scavenger at the best of times, was rooting around in the bushes, so I gave his lead a sharp tug. "Anyway, it's time we headed for home. Enjoy your walk."

My attempt to extricate myself failed. Somehow, as Caliban moved towards me, the woman ended up between us, encircled part way by the lead. I held it out to help her to free herself. "Don't panic," I instructed her. "Don't move. This won't take a second." But in the general confusion she ended up with the lead in her hand, forcing me, accidentally, to let go. She looked at it, nonplussed, then at the dog. He faced her.

"Sit," she commanded suddenly and to my surprise he did. She adjusted her feet with exaggerated care; he tilted his head expectantly. "Good dog." A flash of lightning froze the scene.

I put my hand out to take over, but she changed her hold half teasingly.

"Down," she said.

Caliban lay down.

We both heard the thunder this time.

"Maybe I should get a dog." She paused, seemingly weighing the pros and cons. "What do you think? It would be someone to count on. He wouldn't up and leave me, now, would he?" She glanced at me somewhat belligerently. When I didn't respond, she repeated her commands. "Sit."

81

Caliban sat. "Down." He lay down. "Good boy. It looks like it's your master you'd be prepared to abandon, not me."

I was beginning to feel uncomfortable. "I'm afraid he's not for sale," I told her.

"And you a politician? Oh, but he must be!"

Her laugh did nothing to reassure me; even so, I was flattered to learn that she recognized me.

"Am I right in assuming you're a constituent?"

She raised her hands, as if to ward me off, awkwardly, encumbered by handbag and lead. Had I moved towards her? I backed away. Being misunderstood when seeking to establish rapport with one's potential followers is something of an occupational hazard. Every vote counts and so a close embrace, an understanding smile, a two-handed handshake become essential tools of the trade. Still, they must be handled with care. Like other seasoned politicians I generally shy away from children, who tend to be unpredictable. Kissing a baby is a no-no except in an emergency. If the polls call for desperate measures, I'll face the music, naturally.

She denied it; she was not a constituent. I felt a rush of excitement, gratified at being known beyond the local boundaries.

"I'm here on business." A fleeting smile crossed her face. She quickly bent her head.

I took in the fine black and white check suit, the stylish hat, the rectangular handbag, an outfit which would have been at home in a theatrical wardrobe or fancy dress shop. Was she an actress? Holding my tongue, I deftly sidestepped her claim.

"And ended up in the park all alone?"

"Oh, but I'm not. I'm here with you and Cal."

"You couldn't have known that."

"I couldn't?"

82

She must be more befuddled than I had thought. Or was she being coy? I tried to search her face, but shaded by the brim of her hat it gave nothing away. A timely flash, accompanied by a peal of thunder, brought no revelation. The storm was closing in on us.

Within seconds, it seemed, there was a surge of wind, flattening bushes and grass, bending the trees. A man came running out of nowhere, clutching his jacket with one hand to keep it from flapping. He shouted something and was gone. "There's a hell…" was all I caught; the wind made away with the rest.

"We'd better find shelter," said the woman as the rain began to fall. "If I'm not mistaken, there's a pavilion up ahead. Come, Cal," and she set off with the dog at her side, moving fast in spite of her tipsiness, in spite of the wind.

Less fleet-footed than I used to be, I soon lost sight of them in the semi-darkness. What pavilion had she meant? I knew of a ramshackle building some distance away – would that be it? Trusting that it was, I made my way there through the rain, which soon turned into a downpour. Gazebo-like, consisting of a roof held up by a few posts above a rotting octagonal floor, it would yet provide protection. I'd never been inside, but now, after negotiating the two narrow steps at the opening, whose planks were about to disintegrate, I saw it was a lot bigger than I had imagined – it could easily accommodate a large gathering. Built around a central column was a bench, from which visitors could take in the view. In this weather there was none: the rain curtained off the surroundings. There was a distinctive smell, which I recognized but couldn't place. Light from a streetlamp nearby reached one side of the building but barely penetrated the gloom. The roof modified all sounds. It was eerie, as if I was experiencing the scene at one remove.

A voice stirred me.

"Here, Caliban," I heard, "let's see if we can pull this off."

Caliban?

I got out of my jacket, which was far from waterproof, and shook it, as if that would make the least difference. I spread it out on the bench. A few feet away the woman was down on one knee, her handbag at her side. Either the material in her suit was more water-repellent than mine or else she had escaped the worst of the rainfall – she looked curiously dry. "Down," she commanded and Caliban flopped down. She held her hand in front of him. He sniffed at it. "Roll over." Slowly she made a sweeping motion and he stretched to get to her hand, moving onto his side, straining his neck. "All the way," she ordered, keeping her hand just out of reach. Then he was on his other side and righted his body. "Very good." She gave him whatever it was she had used to tempt him. "You're quite a performer." She patted him.

What happened to the inebriate afraid of dogs?

"He's not the only one," I said.

"Oh, there you are." She got up and brushed down the skirt of her suit. Caliban lay flat, watching her, his nose on top of her bag. "He's a fast learner."

"Caliban."

"Yes."

"I called him Cal."

There was a moment's hesitation. "That was on my account, wasn't it?" she stated. "To make him fit company."

She looked so certain that I chose not to contradict her. "It might have been."

"Because Caliban was a rapist."

"He was?" My surprise was genuine.

"Well, he would have been if Prospero hadn't prevented him. And would have gloated over it. Of course, if you read

84

The Tempest at school, you wouldn't know. The lines that give that information would be omitted. Your teacher would have labelled him a noble savage."

The rain pounded on the roof in the pause that followed. Surely she must be wrong? Somehow she had become the prosecutor, I the defendant. But who or what was I to defend? Caliban? Myself for having picked a tarnished name? My school's use of an expurgated version of the play?

"I'll rename him Prospero, shall I?" I asked, in order to please her.

Her silence was eloquent. Cal, Caliban, Caligula, it said. It's not the name that is at issue. It's what it represents.

And I knew what that was.

Male chauvinism.

Was my conclusion premature? What came next sounded wistful rather than reproving. "For me," she said, "there was no Prospero."

Then I caught on. I fingered my jacket, straightening one of the sleeves. "Well, life's no fairy tale," I offered. I'm no father confessor, as I've already pointed out.

There was a flash and in the same instant, it seemed, a tremendous crash. Lightning must have struck close by. Was I safe?

"I hope there's a lightning rod," I remarked.

She echoed my statement: "Life's no fairy tale," then turned her back on me and stared out at the rain that had not let up in the least. Was she thinking of braving the elements? It would be foolhardy – we were right in the centre of the storm. But if that had been her intention, she changed her mind. When she continued, what she said had nothing to do with our predicament. Instead she placed herself in a world peopled by Calibans.

"It goes without saying that what he did, my Caliban,

85

wouldn't have been considered rape – if I'd dared tell someone." Her words barely reached me. Then she spun around and her voice grew louder. "Well, not much has changed: the situation is the same today. When a man rapes a woman, it's her fault for leading him on." She broke off, but I knew better than to respond. Whatever I came up with was not what she would hear.

"I was in love with him," she said after a long pause. "I just didn't want what he wanted. Not then. I was sixteen. Perhaps not ever. I didn't really trust him. And I was right. Within a week he ditched me for my best friend and did it to her too. He forced himself on her as he had forced himself on me. Only she was luckier; she didn't end up pregnant."

She glared at me, I saw, as the next flash lit up the stage where we stood motionless, opposite one another – for that was how it felt: we were on stage. All that was missing was an audience. The crash, when it came, did nothing to remove that impression – it had the impact of a cymbal in an empty room, a well-timed sound effect.

"Her name was Helen," she added, as if it mattered – a common enough name in any neighbourhood, but one that, in my case, was of special significance: I once had a brief but intense relationship with a girl called Helen. The muted sound of the rain filled the space between us as my mind went into overdrive. Triggered by the name in combination with the curious circumstances of our meeting, I was groping for answers to questions that as yet had to take shape. Where was the woman headed? Should I steer her off course before she arrived at her goal?

"For a while," she said, interrupting my attempt to come to a decision, "I blamed her. If it hadn't been for her, he would have stayed with me – that was how I reasoned. As if that would have cancelled out what he had done! Besides, he left her too, after he got what he wanted." She looked briefly at Caliban, who lay transfixed. I hadn't seen him so relaxed in a long time. Unlike me, he must have found her voice soothing.

"And I blamed myself."

Again I was surprised. Few women will admit that they are in any way responsible. I praised her open-mindedness. "You're right there. It takes two." I nodded, prematurely, as her rejoinder showed.

"Master and slave, you mean. Or if not quite a slave, then paralysed by fear of what might happen to her if she were to fight back. No." She shook her head. "I blamed myself for having trusted him. I blamed myself for letting him come close. I blamed myself for not having inflicted as much damage as I could."

Her tone was calm, matter-of-fact. She walked over to the railing and put her hands on it. Then she turned around.

"But most of all, naturally," she said, "I blamed the one who did it: you."

Afterwards, I could see that everything had led up to that statement: her theatrical outfit, her feigned drunkenness, her professed fear, each intended to arouse my interest – even the thunderstorm, though none of her doing, played its part, sealing us off from any passers-by while making escape well-nigh impossible. At the time there was no room for reflection, but I sensed, nonetheless, that obsession was at the heart of her actions and obsession has to be treated with caution. I was in two minds about what to do. Should I insist she had the wrong man? What might she not do if I tried to swear myself free? My career, if nothing else, was at stake. Bide your time, I told myself. Soon the storm will subside. We will move on. And true enough, the interval between lightning and thunder doubled and then trebled; the rain eased off at least temporarily.

87

"I wished I could have someone come and rape you," she told me. "I played the scene out almost daily. I had you cringing. I had you plead for mercy. But then I lost track of you, oh, years ago. It was only recently, thanks to the Internet, that I located you. I'm sure you've changed, but to me you look the same."

I accepted the compliment unthinkingly.

She paused, wrapped up in her own world. Was she at all amenable to reason? "You mentioned Prospero," I reminded her. "From what little I remember of the play, it's about forgiveness." I waited, expectantly.

She brushed aside my indirect plea. "I used to teach it." She looked up, as if I had expressed doubts. "Yes, I was a teacher. But I taught it differently. What I see in it are women passed on from one man to another, to honour and obey, regardless of their worth. Claribel. Miranda. I see Ferdinand, supposedly a model husband-to-be, cheating Miranda at chess – while courting her. No man can be trusted – that is the lesson of the play. No man is innocent."

Claribel? Fumbling about among cloudy memories I had no argument.

"Now, help me carry Caliban outside." She marched over to the dog, who was lying on his side, his head resting peacefully on her bag.

Faced with her accusations I had forgotten him completely. Why would he have to be carried? I joined her with what speed I could muster and bent down to examine him. He was breathing without effort as dogs do when they are relaxed – I was the one who, crouching down, was short of breath – but he failed to respond to my touch. I looked up at her. "What have you done?"

"He's just asleep," she said. "I gave him a sedative. I followed the vet's instructions to the letter. He'll come to in a while."

"But why?" I kept my voice low. Anger, I have learned, on or off camera, will rarely achieve one's objectives.

"I'll be putting on a display."

She stood over me. Her whole stance challenged me – I found it hard to hold my tongue. "You have been ever since we met," I told her.

But if she heard the note of sarcasm, she didn't let on.

"I'm talking about fireworks," she said. "Dogs often panic if they're exposed to loud noises. A sedative helps."

I got to my feet, awkwardly. Fireworks never bothered Caliban; still, moving him could do no harm. I went to pick him up. He is too heavy by far, but to share the burden with someone I couldn't trust would have been worse. Hoisting him up off the floor was the hardest bit – I lost my balance the first time and had to make a new attempt – but getting down from the pavilion to the ground proved almost as difficult. In the end I had to ease myself down backwards – the steps gave little foothold. Once out in the open I put him down a short distance away under a tree, which was as far as I could carry him. The rain had all but ceased. "Be with you soon," I told him. I stroked his head, his neck.

And as my thumb and forefinger caressed his ear, I was sorely tempted to take off, then and there – but what might she do if I did? To Caliban? To me?

"Why are you doing this?" I asked as I returned. "A fireworks display? During a thunderstorm?"

"It's how they used to do things in India," she said. "Well, more or less. We're not in India." She stopped as if to give me room to say, *Oh, but we are*, but when I didn't, she went on: "Your son—"

And there I did object.

"I have no son."

"You're right. You don't," she conceded. "He died in a car crash three weeks ago."

I did a double take. Pregnant, she had said. I should have paid closer attention. I should have added two and two together. Or better still, I should have fled as soon as I laid eyes on her.

But then she would surely have got to me some other way.

In my mind's eye I saw her going to the press. I saw the front page of the local paper. I saw my inbox filling up with mail. There'd be no evidence, nothing to prove her allegations, but rumours alone can topple any politician. If the boy had been cremated, as seemed likely after a car crash, there'd be no DNA – unless she had kept them, the ashes would presumably have been spread to the four winds. Was that what they did in India? There'd be no proof either way. I saw the result of the polls. Under no circumstances could I let her foist a son upon me.

"I'm sorry," I repeated. "Sorry to hear of your loss. But I'm not the one you're after. You're making a mistake."

She didn't yield. "Helen confirmed it," were her words.

There was a late flash of lightning and again, almost immediately, a crash. We scowled at one another. Was the storm starting up again?

"I know no Helen." I looked her straight in the eye. Why complicate matters? "But since I'm here," I said, meeting her part way, "I'll stay for the ceremony you'd planned, out of respect for your grief and to honour your son's memory." I made a half bow. "I owe you that much."

The phrase was out before I realized how inappropriate it was. I should stop speaking as a politician. I owed her nothing – nothing, that is, unless I viewed myself, for the occasion, as a representative of men in general. I chose that reading: she had been wronged, wronged by a man. I fit part of the bill.

"He was how old?" I asked.

But she was moving towards the steps and didn't hear

my question. No matter. It was nothing to me. I saw her reach down and pick something up. Stooping here and there, she circled the perimeter, and as she did, I caught the smell that had been there when I arrived, but now it was more than a whiff. Fireworks, I should have recalled, have a distinctive smell; she must have set them up all around the foundation. I sat down on the bench, ready to enjoy myself in spite of the situation – since I was there I might as well watch the show. Soon a light flickered. There was a hissing sound and I adjusted my position for a better view. Then everything went haywire. Instead of zooming outwards and up, towards the sky, the rocket she had lit struck a different course, hitting the ceiling. Within seconds it fell to the floor and there it exploded. Sparks flew everywhere. It took a while before I managed to stamp on what was left of it and save the planks from catching fire.

When I was done, I saw to my alarm that she had lit a second rocket, a few feet further on. How many were there? Eight? Ten? Twelve? "Don't!" I shouted, but too late. Had she failed to notice what had happened? "The wind's too strong!" I yelled. "It isn't safe!" The second firework followed the same course as the first, landing close to me, but I was out of breath from shouting and took longer to get there. When I stomped on it, frustrated with her carelessness, I felt the floorboard cave in under my foot. There was no pain, but I suspected I had sprained my ankle. To avoid making matters worse, I limped back to the bench.

What had looked like an accident was deliberate, I understood – but I had yet to note the full extent of her machinations. Not until I saw the smoke that had begun to wind itself around the posts that supported the roof, wafting in under the rafters, did I catch on. As I did, a sharp fizzle told me she had just set off a third – or, had I missed one? – a fourth firework. I was no longer able to think clearly.

Too much was going on. Rockets were igniting the floor. Flames were licking the part of the railing she had passed.

How could it burn after all that rain?

I knew I had to get out fast. Although the posts on one side of the opening were on fire, the entrance, I decided, despite its crumbling steps, offered a safer escape than if I were to crawl under the railing somewhere else to make it to the ground. I got to my feet unsteadily but have no clear memory of what happened next. My eyes were smarting from the smoke; I held a hand over my mouth and nose to avoid breathing it in. I must have crossed the floor, dragging one foot behind me. Nothing stopped me until I felt a hand tugging at my arm from behind. A voice shouted something. I wrenched myself free. "You're not getting away!" I heard. "Not this time!" In the same instant the first two posts collapsed, causing part of the roof to fall in. All hell broke loose.

The incident made no headlines. In part this was no doubt because the police kept my name out of it, as someone who had happened on the scene due to the storm; in part because it was an open-and-shut case. The cans that had held the petrol had been bought at a local service station; the buyer was a woman whose description matched the deceased. Her name meant nothing to me. No long drawn-out investigation was called for. It was a clear instance of self-immolation.

I suffered only minor burns.

"It wouldn't have been you she was after, now, would it?" one of the officers joked at a summing-up session.

I laughed. "A mere politician? What did we ever do to anyone?"

I picked up Caliban from the sergeant at the reception desk and we set out together for the park. It was late afternoon. As we approached the site where the pavilion had stood, I pondered the question that had weighed on my mind the last few days: had her Helen really been mine? To be quite truthful, I had come to wonder if mine had even been called Helen. I've mixed up names before. It could have been Ethel. It could have been Ellen. The stressful situation would explain the mix-up – that's human nature. Deep in thought, I detoured the disorderly pile of what remained of posts, rafters and roofing; the smell of burning was strong even now. Helen? It didn't sound right. I stopped with my back to the scene and took in the view. There were no clouds on the horizon. There was nothing to disturb the tranquillity I had come to find.

"Sit, Caliban," I said and Caliban sat. "Down." He lay down. I left it at that. I saw no need for him to learn any more tricks.

This Is for You

"Listen to this," he says. He runs his hand along the strings inside the old upright, making it sound like a harp but with more of a twang. "You hear?"

Gerald never took lessons.

"Were you polishing it?" Joan asks. He has folded back the top. It is divided in two, lengthwise; four hinges hold the sections together. This is the first time she has seen him near it.

"No. I was wondering what it looked like inside."

"There are strings and hammers," she tells him.

"I know that. I wanted a peep."

Sometimes he is so childlike.

It is his piano. Joan never wanted it. When his uncle died, no one had any use for it so Gerald took it. "I'll learn to play next year when I retire," he had said, always the optimist. She had objected, pointing out how big it was: it would dwarf everything in the room. If he wanted an instrument, he could get one of those small digital keyboards that were so popular. But he had made up his mind and she yielded. At least it was better than the choice of some retirees she has heard of, a Harley-Davidson, if only just – with its cast iron frame it no doubt weighs about the same. It is stationary, though. He won't kill himself rounding some curve. At the funeral, where the shiny black coffin, surrounded by wreaths and flowers, reminded her of the piano, she'd thought she might be able to hide it behind a wall of aspidistras, creating an indoor bower of sorts that she need never visit.

Actually, what troubled her was less its size than the memories that surfaced with it, tainting its arrival, but this she did not tell him. Unlike Gerald, she had taken lessons as a child. No older than eleven or twelve, she had had no say in the matter. Had she but known, a clichéd phrase she learned appeared with some frequency in the whodunnits that her parents read; had she but known what would follow, what crime, for so she viewed it, would be perpetrated on her, she might have – indeed, she would have – put up a fight. Not that it would have helped. She was at that in-between stage of no resistance, neither small enough to be able to resort to temper tantrums at home and abroad, shaming her parents into backing down, nor yet a teenager combining the will of a two-year-old with the strength of an adult. But she did not know.

Oh, the bitterness that the instrument evokes.

She leaves Gerald playing at playing and goes out into the garden. There is weeding to be done, a more congenial five-finger exercise that might take her mind off the drills she suffered through as a child. Gloved, she picks up a trowel and gets a cushion; she works diligently, kneeling as she starts out but soon half-seated, to save her knees. Whatever she does not recognize, whatever comes without a name, she treats as a weed. Before long there is a small pile beside her.

It does not help, though.

If she could put her memories in a pile and bury them, that might.

Miss Griffith – that was her name. Funny how some names stick. Or was it Griffiths? No, Griffith. A mouthful either way. Not that Joan had had to use the name; yes, miss, no, miss was all that was required.

Yes, miss. No, miss. Yes, miss, I'll try.

The last, modified version she learned to avoid. Whether or not Miss Griffith was familiar with Matthew 5, any attempt to qualify a yes or no was quickly stifled: "... let your communication be, Yea, yea; Nay, nay..." Vulture-like – was that really true? – her cold eyes signalled disapproval. There was no need for words to reinforce the message.

Joan shivers, less at some actual memory than at the picture she has conjured up. She takes off her gloves to move a strand of hair out of her face before going back to weeding.

But the image of her teacher returns.

The early sessions left little trace. What she had to learn was relatively simple: brief exercises and a few tunes long since familiar. Reading music was new, naturally, but appeared uncomplicated: a mere fraction of the keyboard was used – her hands, and mostly only one initially, were kept within the confines of one octave; there were no sharps or flats; each note was one, two or four beats, nothing more complex; and though their names must have been used, crotchet, minim, whatever, she had paid scant attention so they never bothered her.

But over time, as the lessons progressed, she herself failed to do so. What she remembers from the years that followed is her own ineptitude – and Miss Griffith's impatience.

"Stop," she would say. "Stop right there. Your whole body is tense. You must learn to relax." She would grab Joan's hand. "Your wrists have to be supple." And to achieve the desired suppleness she would bash the offending hand against the keys, keeping time with her command: "Relax. Relax. Relax."

But how could Joan relax? When the music in front of her had the appearance of a minefield, each note a mine, its position at times confused by sharps and flats to be found not where the note stood but to the far left, by the clef; when each note or chord had its own value, forcing her to keep count; when some had additional symbols attached to them, adding or cancelling information; when often whole sets of notes had escaped the lines that held the rest and were to be found high above or far below them, on a separate line or set of lines, to indicate – and force her to calculate – its place in the system, as if she had nothing else to do – how could she relax?

Even at home, where she had time to figure out, pencil in hand, which key to press down, she was likely to go wrong. What sounded fine to her was very often not what the composer had intended. "D?" Miss Griffith would say, her intonation stressing the absurdity of what she had heard. "D? Where do you find that?" And not too sure exactly where she had played a D, Joan's hand would hover while she searched the field until Miss Griffith grabbed it and made it land on the keyboard in the vicinity of the A she should have played, resulting in both pain and dissonance.

Joan stabs at a root. Too late she sees it is an aster, not a weed. She shrugs. The asters can do with thinning anyway. She starts a second pile beside the weeds. Once she is done, she'll pick a few to bring indoors.

Mistakes, she knows, will happen if you are in a rush, in music as in gardening. Strange that she never simply took it in her stride. At school, she was fed the teacherly platitude used to pat slow learners on the back: you can't improve unless you make mistakes. Miss Griffith proffered no consolation. Would it have helped Joan if she had, or, alternatively, if her mistakes had been ignored? Joan doubts it. When her fingers got entangled; when she very obviously hit the wrong note; when she was completely stuck, she knew, and knowing never shrugged it off as a necessary step in order to learn. Pieces marked *adagio* and *lento* she could negotiate, if barely. But with tempos like *allegro* and *vivace*, even though Miss Griffith spared her the metronome, she grew hot and uncomfortable, playing as if she was wearing mittens on both hands. And *allegrissimo*, if she had ever had the misfortune to

97

encounter it, would have made her bury her musical trowel full force in the nearest hornets' nest.

What Miss Griffith did not spare her was playing four-handed, a cruel exercise, always involving music she had neither seen nor heard before. "Would you move over to the left, please," Miss Griffith would say and Joan knew immediately what she was in for. Why did the left page, with the lower pitch, generally the bass, always fall on her? There were fewer notes to play and fewer complicated sequences, it is true, but as a consequence there were also a great many places where she had to pause for one or more beats, long rests indicated by dashes suspended from or reposing on the line, as if that could make much difference, short ones by squiggles that caused problems of their own. When was she to play the next note? She never knew. She never knew till the moment Miss Griffith slowed down markedly to spur her on and then, not hiding her exasperation, drew to a halt. And as if those problems were not enough, more notes than ever were submerged in the depths, far below the few she had finally learned to master, secured as they were on or between the lines – though to claim mastery was perhaps wishful thinking. As often as not she still missed sharps and flats.

"What key are we playing in?" Miss Griffith would ask and Joan would know that that was not the question.

"D?" she would suggest, a common key.

"So where do you find that?"

Joan's eyes would roam in search of a letter that might be the key to the key.

The prompt would be terse.

"Look at the last note."

Often there wasn't one. "There are three," she would say, looking at the chord, her confusion growing.

"You go by the bass note."

"A," she would say.

G it would be.

"And how many sharps are there in G major?"

Two? Three? Joan would guess wildly, even though she knew. She really did.

All that to tell her she had played an F instead of an F#. And so it went.

Joan looks at the flower in her left hand, where there should have been a weed. The humiliation she felt is with her even today, after so many years. She was ignorant, no two ways about it, and made to feel more so – made to remain the weed she was. Unable to focus clearly, she looks at the pile she has been adding to and finds more asters there: three... four... five. She shouldn't get so involved in the past. Gently she separates them from the weeds and places them beside the flower she cut down first. Perhaps she will be able to transplant a few from places where they grow too close and fill the gaps.

Predictably, with hindsight, her reaction had been to resort to subterfuge. She feels bad about this too: wiliness is not a trait she admires – well, who does? – but has her defence prepared. She was trying to protect herself. Nor did she turn into a hardened criminal, playing truant, defiantly. Twice, twice, that was all, she made use of a stratagem, telling her parents she had hurt her wrist – the wrist not supple enough for Miss Griffith – by falling, being pushed, in the gym. No need for details. No need for a doctor either; most likely it was no more than a sprain. She would be fine in a few weeks. And she was – until the next time, less than a year later. What unwilling piano pupil has not done the same?

Joan pulls at a root that is protruding from the edge of the flowerbed in order to remove it. It won't yield, so she hacks at it, repeating Miss Griffith's exercise to get her to loosen up. Weeding might have made her a better pianist.

She smiles but dismisses the thought. Practice might have. A reluctant pupil, she often put off practising as long as possible, if not in fact entirely. As a result, once or twice, never routinely, she had presented the previous week's assignment as her new homework – Miss Griffith had so many pupils that she was unlikely to keep track of them all. Had she even erased the date on one or two occasions, the date Miss Griffith generally pencilled beside the title of a new piece? She is not sure. She pats down the soil where the root had been.

Enough for today. Joan lets go of the trowel, gathers the weeds in her arms and takes them to the compost bin. When she returns, she removes her gloves. She picks up the seven asters that fell victim to her inattentiveness. Tomorrow she will try and move some that are still in bud to fill their places. It might work.

Inside, there is no Gerald – he must have gone out the front. She leaves the flowers beside the sink and heads for the living room. There the top of the piano is still open. She walks over to close it but changes her mind. Instead she pulls out the stool, sits down and lifts the lid that covers the keys. There are eighty-eight of them, she knows, where twenty-four, two octaves, would have kept her busy – perhaps even content.

Could things have worked out differently? No prodigy, could she have learned to play? There is no knowing. It is easy to blame Miss Griffith. She was the teacher, and the adult. But where were Joan's parents? Why didn't they see what was going on and put a stop to it? More to the point, why didn't she herself speak up? Or did she? She must have complained, surely, or was she too well brought up, too well-behaved? Is that the reason she lied, and went on lying, about her homework? Well-behaved and devious both.

Frustrated she hits the keys with her two hands

100

simultaneously, her wrists not the least relaxed, producing a clamour, a cacophony of sound. She pushes down on the sustain pedal with her right foot and keeps it down, hitting the keys a second time, a third. "This is for you," she says, and then repeats the phrase again and again, louder and louder, ending up shouting at the top of her voice while pounding the keys, no longer knowing who she is addressing: "This is for you! This is for you!" Not until she is out of breath does she stop. She slumps over the keyboard. The echo lingers.

When she looks up, Gerald is standing in the doorway.

"I'll get rid of it," he says, quietly.

"It's all right," she tells him. "It won't happen again. I'm done."

And she gets up. The flowers in the kitchen will need water. She has to find them a vase. At least she can do that much.

loss.doc

He answers the phone on the fourth ring. It is his mother.

"It's over," she says. "He passed away early this morning."

She waits, but what can he say? Andrew had looked in last night, but his father had not wanted to talk. There was a TV set in the room, a room he had to himself, with a film running. What was it called? Andrew had seen it a few years ago, but all he could remember was the closing scene with the frogs. And the soundtrack – Aimee Mann at her best. His mother had stayed at the hospital, but he had gone home, turned off the phone. Today is his day off.

"The funeral will be in about a week. You will come, won't you?"

He hesitates.

"I can't really see the point."

"It's customary. You bury people when they die."

"There's no need to be sarcastic. You know what I mean."

"I'd like to see you there," she says.

Does he make some sort of promise? He is not sure.

It has come as no surprise. His father has been in hospital no more than a week, but the reason he was admitted was that there wasn't much time left. There was no cure. The cancer had spread. The chemotherapy hadn't worked. Radiotherapy would have been pointless at this stage. All that could be provided was palliative care, they said, which basically meant shots of morphine.

Sister Morphine, he'd thought when his mother told him.

Had he been callous? Probably. But the thought had been automatic, not a response to the situation. It isn't that he lives his life through music, keeping reality at one remove, so to speak; at least he doesn't think so. All the same, when pop music is a constant presence in your life, is it any wonder that it makes itself known? "Is it any wonder," he hums. Call it callous, if you like.

At the same time, it wasn't that he had been happy that his father was dying, that he is now dead. Death is no laughing matter. Is that from some song too? Truly, he had felt very little. In part, of course, this was because he had known for quite some time where things were headed. And in part it was because he had never really been close to his father. Theirs was not a tactile relationship, as someone – Clapton? – said about himself and *his* father – who turned out not to be that. Andrew's father was never physical either, other than possibly to cuff him when he saw the need for it. There was always a distance between them.

Andrew isn't sure that never and always are the right words, though. What he does know is that he became acutely conscious of that distance when he was fourteen and saw his classmates, or at least one of them, with *his* father. Those two were friends. They talked to each other. They laughed. They touched.

It was at about that time, he remembers, that he became convinced that his father wasn't his father somehow, long before he had read anyone's autobiography, least of all Clapton's, and long before he knew that this is a common fantasy among children. Or is it only among boys? He's not sure. As a result, though it might have happened anyway, he'd spent a lot of time in front of the mirror, examining his face. He saw no resemblance. True, they both had brown hair and blue eyes, but his father's eyes were a darker shade. Would Andrew's nose and ears end up looking like his father's? It was in part vanity that made him deny that, but also the fact that it really seemed impossible: his father's ears and nose were so much bigger. Could gravity do that to you, given time? He had looked through an old photo album for evidence, but found no pictures of his father in his teens. Didn't people have cameras in those days? There was a studio shot of his father in his mid-twenties, probably, but he looked nothing like a cross between the two of them, as he ought to have done.

Andrew cannot really recall how it had come about, but it was then, too, that he began to daydream that Mr. Brooks, his English teacher, was his father. Mr. Brooks showed an interest in him. He saw him.

"Andrew," he would say when they were on their way out of the classroom, or "Andy". And Andy would be waiting for this to turn into "Andy, my boy" or, simply, "son". "I liked your comments today. They were perceptive."

"Thank you, sir."

"You're a good reader. Keep it up."

"Yes, sir."

And at night, when he went to bed, he would fantasize not about how they had met, his mother and Mr. Brooks, nor how they had come to part – be cruelly parted? – before – or was it after? – Andrew was born, but how Mr. Brooks would reveal to him one day that he was his father. Initially there were several versions, but they came to solidify into one, which never quite reached its conclusion. He was always asleep before he got that far.

Of course, had he been a bit older or more used to the ways of the world, or perhaps less in need, he would have seen much sooner what Brooks was after – which must have been, to use that curiously formal phrase, a tactile relationship. When he did see; when he could not but see, he had felt betrayed. Even worse, he had felt stupid. How could he have been so blind? What a fool he had been! If anybody found out, he would never hear the end of it. That had been his reaction then; now, so much older, he is a different person, but even so, it is not an episode he talks about. If he were to write his autobiography, he would leave it out. That is not about to happen, though. His place in the music industry is less than peripheral – very much off the fringe – so no publisher will be putting in a bid for his life.

Andrew gets up from his desk, which is where he took the call, and makes himself coffee. He feels slightly hungover. This must be largely due to lack of sleep; he hadn't had that much to drink. Instead of returning to the desk he sinks down in an armchair.

Brooks deserves some credit, though, he thinks. If it hadn't been for his encouragement, he might have had even less confidence in himself. His father certainly never took an interest in what he did or what he wanted to do, whether it concerned pets or music. Of course he hadn't shown any special talent, but how could he when there were no instruments around? Surely his determination to join a band should have counted for something. Nor had he been unrealistic: he knew he didn't have much of a voice, but bass players were not expected to be lead singers. And an instrument with four strings should be fairly easy to handle. He could surely learn some simple lines, which was what most bass players did. But even that had not convinced his father. He had never supported him in any activity.

Now you're being unfair, he hears his father say. *I tried to get you to join the Boys' Brigade, but you refused. That would have given you lots of friends. I took you to the seaside. I—*

Once, he breaks in. *And when we were there, you lost me.*

That was your doing. You were the one who wandered off.

I was six. You should have kept an eye on me.

105

I told you to stay out of the water. I told you to stay around. Besides, you came to no harm.

No thanks to you, he says.

But what's the point? He sips at his coffee. You can't argue with a dead man.

A good title, that.

The distance that is, that was, between them bothered him, though. Of course it had been far-fetched to suspect – to hope, really – that he was an illegitimate child; it spoke only of his longing. What he knew of his mother should have put an end to such fantasies. She was thirty-four when he was born and hardly likely to have fallen madly in love with someone who had then vanished. Nobody would describe her as passionate. Andrew had wanted to ask her, but couldn't, of course, not even indirectly.

What was it like, dating someone, when you were young?

What do you mean?

Well, for instance, did you...

Did you do what? Did you do things you shouldn't do? That was not the kind of question you could ask your mother. There were really no questions that would have led to the answer he was looking for.

Did you do your dating in a car?

Did you end up where the moonbeams are?

A bit too close to Neil Young, but not without potential. Star. Went too far.

No, he had never asked her. What he had asked, and that was later, was not about herself. What was the occasion? Was it the first time one of his songs made a brief appearance on the charts? Well, it had been Jeff's song as well, of course; he had written the music and Andrew knows that for most people the music matters more than the lyrics. He had expected a pat on the back from his father,

106

but his only comment was "So I heard" before he disappeared into the yard. "So I heard." This was after Andrew had sweated for he did not know how long over lyrics that took him nowhere and then waited interminably for someone to record the song. "So I heard." Not even a pat on the back. Out of his frustration he had turned to his mother.

"Did he ever even hold me?" he had asked.

"Hold you?" she had said. "Why should he hold you?"

Would that have been so strange? What kind of family was this?

"Some fathers do, don't they?"

"When you were little, you mean? Of course he did. He must have. Well, he wasn't home much. And when he was, you were mostly asleep. But of course he must have held you."

He had waited, far from convinced. And then she had laughed.

"I remember once when he shouldn't have."

"He shouldn't?"

"It was early in the morning. You probably had a bit of a nappy rash, so I'd left you to air for a minute."

"And he held me?"

"He was still in bed and lifted you up, above his head. Well, you can imagine what happened."

"What?"

"Never mind," she had said. "I shouldn't have brought it up."

But she had been right. He can imagine the scene: There is a child crying – himself – and a woman – his mother – saying, *Shh baby, I hear you. Don't wake Daddy. I'm coming.* She gets out of bed, picks him up. *There,* she says. *Let me get this wet nappy off.* Then she feeds him – bottle? breast? – this is a part he skips – and finishes off by burping

107

him. At that point, his father, now awake, offers to hold him while she goes to get a nappy. In the worst-case scenario – he likes to dramatize the incident – his father is lying on his back. He juggles him in the air, saying something like, *Who's a big boy, then?*

That is when it happens.

And what did his father do? Did he turn his face, his head, quickly, making a sound halfway between a snort and a cough, rolling, almost falling, out of bed, holding him, Andrew, at arm's length? Take him! Performed with speed, that would test anyone's agility. Or did he simply drop him? *You little sod! I'll…!*

Why had he offered to hold him at all? If this was the only occasion his mother could remember, it must have been rare not only in what happened, but overall. Was he in a particularly good mood? Was it a Sunday or a holiday, since he was still around and in no hurry to get up? Only to be rewarded thus!

Poor man. Andrew shakes his head.

The incident does not explain the distance between them, though; his father can hardly have blamed him for something so accidental. And Andrew never knowingly peed on him, metaphorically speaking. If he disappointed him, it was by going his own way, not by doing the dirty on him, to vary the metaphor. True, his day job was not one his father approved of. Chosen so as to leave time and energy for his song writing, it mostly consisted of working nights in hospitals and mental institutions as a porter or attendant. But then, children rarely follow in their parents' footsteps, do they? What could be more natural than a gap between generations? I'm a child of the sixties, he thinks, though he's not. I don't go with the flow.

Of course, all the others in the family did; not one of them struggled upstream. Brian, Kevin, Susan, Frank, Jeanette – all

108

the cousins on his mother's side lived up to their parents' expectations. Had his father not been an only child, had Andrew had more cousins, they would probably have been equally conservative. When Brian and company were too busy to turn up for family gatherings, their parents always reported on their progress, generally finishing on the same note. Our investment's paid off, it said: he – or she – has done us proud. This is a phrase Andrew detests. His father, of course, had had no reason to use it: it was reserved for those who weren't there. But if Andrew hadn't been there, would he? Did he resent the fact that he couldn't?

I don't see my lack of success as failing you, he says. *But if it is, then the failing was surely mutual.*

He is not at all sure what his father's reply would have been. This isn't something they ever talked about.

His coffee is cold, but he drinks it anyway.

There are of course any number of questions that he never asked, mostly because he didn't feel he could. "I should have asked you," sings Emmylou Harris on one of her albums, or something to that effect, giving voice to a character whose father isn't around anymore, but unlike her, Andrew never meant to. He has no list of questions.

What would have topped such a list?

The answer comes in a flash.

Did you actually want *me?*

Is that the most fundamental one?

And what would his father have replied? Would he have avoided the issue? Probably.

Times were different.

Then he would most likely have picked up a paper or turned on the TV. Or is Andrew being unfair?

How is that relevant? Andrew would have said, persisting. And then, perhaps, there would have been an attempt at an explanation.

109

I accepted you. I kept you in food and clothing.

But that wasn't really an answer. Andrew would have had to persevere.

Times were different, his father might have repeated then. *Women wanted children. Men, well. You basically accepted that it happened. Or you didn't. I did.*

Is that true? Andrew is confused. Of course men's roles have changed. But...

What you're saying is...

I didn't know how to be a father. I never had one. He died when I was two.

Now, that is a different matter but not much of an excuse. Andrew finds it hard to hold back the bitterness he feels.

I know. And so, as a consequence, neither have I.

I may not have been a good father, his father would have said, but I was there. And believe it or not, I did care.

Did he? Had he? Even in an imagined conversation, or perhaps particularly in an imagined conversation, Andrew can't refrain from having the last word: *You could have fooled me*, he says.

But of course, there is no way he would have asked his father any of those questions. And probably there is no way his father would have answered them.

A line from a song comes to mind: John Lennon grieving for the mother that wasn't there. "Daddy, don't go," Andrew sings, making the necessary substitution. "Daddy, don't go." It is too late for that now, but Lennon too had been late, very late.

That is what he should do: write a song.

Andrew gets up and goes over to the desk to switch on the PC, then to the kitchenette. He needs more coffee. Getting ideas can be painfully slow. There is little in the fridge, he sees. He will need to do some shopping too.

"Father, oh father," he improvises as he makes the coffee, "where did you go? Father, oh father, I miss you so." Tacky, definitely tacky. The sentiment is all right, but not the words.

"New words," he calls out, balancing the mug in his left hand. "New words for old." This is going to be good.

He opens a new file and looks at the screen without seeing it. Father. Father. Daddy. Dad. Pop. Papa. My old man. Gone, gone, gone. Out of reach. Out of sight. Out of mind. Was it Dylan who was asked early in his career if he used a rhyming dictionary and answered something like: "A what? Is there one? You're kidding me!" But a rhyming dictionary has never proved a good starting point. He needs an idea, not a rhyme. And he has to keep it simple, simple and general. What he needs specifically is the opening line or the opening lines. Once he has those Jeff will have to join him.

The file that he has opened is as empty as his mind.

He sips at his coffee.

Empty, empty. Empty streets. Empty rooms. Feeling empty, being empty, running on empty, being left behind.

"He left me here in shadow and went on ahead," he writes. Ahead to do what? Ahead, where? He deletes it. Heaven might be good for business, but it is not a direction he wants to take.

"Someone to lean on," he writes.

"Someone to turn to."

"Someone to…"

If he can develop this, it could form part of the chorus. It needs a final line, though.

This is harder than he had expected. Hard. Harder. Hardest.

"The hardest thing," he writes, "is having to let go."

He feels a rush of excitement. "The hardest thing is

111

having to let go." What a great line! And then he almost freezes. It is surely too good not to have been used before.

Reluctantly he googles it, but to his relief there are only a few matches, and none related to lyrics. This is amazing.

But then he is stuck. He still needs a good first line for the opening verse, but to get that he has to have the situation clear in his mind. It is one of loss, of course, but how get that across without being tearful? He stares at the screen. The cursor winks at him, mechanically, with no intent. Blink, blink rather than wink, wink.

He times it, but soon loses track, looking from screen to watch to see when the sixty seconds are up. He starts again, holding his watch up in front of him, then double-checks. The cursor blinks fifty times per minute, a little slower than his pulse. He times that too, and it is sixty, as it should be. Has the cursor been set at a lower rate to have a calming effect? If so, that is not how he reacts, at least not now. Can he reset it? Can he increase the pace and with it the stress in order to be more creative? He imagines the tests that must have been done to achieve maximum efficiency. There must have been hundreds of subjects working at different tasks, with cursors at different settings. What if the optimal setting had been one that varied according to the subject's eye movements, for instance? Would that have proved too expensive to introduce into the program?

Twinkle, twinkle, little star. Bowie wonders who you are.

This just isn't working, he decides. His imagination is running away with him, which is all well and good, but what comes up is nothing he can use. He has made some sort of start at least. Now he might as well do his shopping, so he can fix lunch. Quickly he saves the file with its skeleton chorus – loss.doc – shuts down the program, switches off the PC. He knows there won't be much point in trying later today; he needs something specific to kick-start him, a scene or a situation of some kind to get him going, something that is both specific and general at the same time. It will come to him, he is quite sure.

And then it strikes him – where is this more likely to happen than at the funeral? It should provide him both with the concrete details that he needs and a whole array of feelings. He sees before him the coffin and the flowers. He sees the shafts of light streaming through the windows. He hears the music. He hears sombre voices. How blind can you be? Without the least hesitation, he moves his hand from the keyboard to the phone. It is time he called his mother back.

What Is There to Say?

No curtains frame the bed – this is a private room. You are sitting on one side, your son and daughter on the other. Your daughter is the one who arrived last – there are no trains at night from where she lives, nor does she have a car. When she pushed the door open, cautiously, your son got up to fetch another chair and she took his. He is now close to the foot of the bed but still has an unobstructed view. The head of the bed is raised at a 45-degree angle.

This is not the picture that you see, of course – yours is more limited. You rarely even look across the bed but have your eyes fixed on your husband.

There has been no change. His skin is pallid but no more than it was a few hours ago. His eyes remain wide open and unseeing. He doesn't blink. After each breath there is a pause, unvaried in length. The tubes are there, as they have been all week: thin ones that run to his nostrils from behind his ears and are connected to the wall outlet for oxygen via a thicker one curled up peacefully on his chest; a catheter that forms a loop at the side of the bed before it disappears out of view. Hospital corners hold the bedclothes in place.

"Will you be back in the morning?" he had asked. His eyes followed you as you prepared to leave in the late afternoon.

You had been, every morning, for the last six days, so there was no need for his question, nor for an answer. You nodded, gave him a hug, making sure you kept clear of all tubes. You didn't turn around in the doorway. You knew he would go back to watching TV or just rest. At this point you regret that you did not – a minor regret, as regrets go, to be followed, no doubt, by countless others. That must be one of the consequences of death.

For a moment you take your eyes off your husband and

114

peer at your son and daughter, wondering how they will cope.

"He loved you very much," you say, keeping your voice down.

You are embarrassed when you realize that you used the past tense. What if he can hear you?

"Still does, I'm sure," you add, though the idea that he should have strong feelings for others at this stage seems almost absurd. You squeeze his hand; you have been holding it since you sat down. You no longer expect a response and there is none.

"Mum, don't," says your daughter.

"Don't what?" you ask.

"Don't treat us like children."

"I don't," you say.

"You know you do."

You shrug.

"Well, to me you do."

Your son frowns.

"Stop it. Both of you."

He is right – this is neither the time nor place – but nonetheless, you are annoyed; you shift a little in your chair in remonstrance. As you do, you notice that the trapeze-like handle that used to be above the bed is gone; the pole that holds it has been swung around and is kept flush against the wall. No one will reach for it, of course. Your husband will not lift himself up or adjust his position ever again. You blink to keep back the tears, for though you knew, it hurts. To calm yourself you fix your gaze on the tubes, grey against the white of the gown. You look intently at the pillow, clean but creased, sporting lines like those in the palm of one's hand, held down by his weight – what little weight there is.

"Did you have supper before you set off?" You steal a

115

glance at your daughter as you ask the question, not quite facing her. She has grown thinner, hasn't she? "You have to eat, no matter what."

"Mum, I'm twenty-eight."

"Still."

"Not again." Your son stands up, catching his chair before it hits the floor. "I have to get some air."

He can open the window, you say, but he is gone.

Your daughter ignores you.

Time moves slowly. Your son returns. He doesn't say where he has been. Other than that there are no interruptions. No nurse peeks in, no doctor, though one must be on call. "It won't be long," was the message you received a little after six o'clock; you had just finished your own supper. You had been surprised: nothing had indicated that he was getting weaker. It is now nearly one. You have been here for well over five hours, as has your son; your daughter close on three.

"Who brought you?" You had not thought to ask. "Clive, was it?"

"Why Clive? I haven't seen him for ages."

"He was nice."

"Mum."

But the point is worth making.

"I know," you say. "I liked him, though. You should have—"

"Mum!"

The interruption comes from both of them this time, like a voice with a built-in echo.

You wonder again how much he can hear, if anything. His eyes reveal nothing, nor does his body stir beyond the slight movement caused by the five or six breaths he takes each minute, so quiet, so calm as to be almost imperceptible. Should you try talking to him? If you did, what could you say? What do night nurses talk about when they watch over a patient?

Perhaps your son's thoughts have gone in the same direction.

"I'd like to be alone with Dad," he says.

"Of course." You try to hide your surprise. "Now?" you ask, in case you have misunderstood him, making assumptions that have nothing to do with his needs.

He nods.

"Not after…"

"No."

"All right."

You let go of your husband's hand and stand up. For a second or two your head spins. This often happens when you get up quickly, but the dizziness never lasts. Your daughter is on her way out. You follow her.

"Come and get us when you're done," you say, hearing as you utter the words that it is the wrong phrase.

The corridor is empty. At one end, in an alcove, is a table with some chairs. Your daughter is on her way there. When you catch up, she has walked over to a window and has her back to you. You join her. Outside the sky is black – you see no moon, no stars. Below, at street level, there is nobody about; there is no traffic at all.

"Does he just want to be with Dad?" you ask.

"I suppose so. Or talk to him. So?"

"Oh, nothing," you say, but that is not what you think. There must be something troubling him but then, why turn to his father? What good will that do at this time?

You sit down at the table. Your daughter remains by the window. Neither of you speaks, but the result is not a comfortable silence.

"Did you offer to pay for the petrol?" you ask.

"Yes," she says.

And had she? She volunteers nothing, but you decide to let it go. Leave her alone, you caution yourself. She doesn't want to talk.

The minutes drag by. There is a clock in the corridor, but if it had not been for the second hand, you would have thought it had stopped. You watch the minute hand. It moves every thirty seconds, soundlessly, and each time trembles slightly in its new position as if the strain involved in getting there had been nearly unbearable. At some point you nod off. When you come to, there is still no sign of your son. Nor is your daughter there.

At two fifteen the door to your husband's room is pulled open and your son comes out to get you. He appears to have been crying, but you are not sure – he may simply have washed his face to stay awake. You do not ask – this is no time for questions – but return to your seat by the bed. The room seems airless after the corridor, but otherwise nothing has changed. Your husband's breathing is as regular as before, his eyes equally lifeless. You take his hand, again hold it in yours.

As in a dream, you hear your daughter's voice, "I tried to find a coffee machine." You must have nodded off. Half asleep, you check your watch and see that it is almost three – at least you are getting through the night. You reproach yourself at the thought. That is not what this is about. But what it is about is not something you want to face.

"Was there one?" you ask.

But she had only come across a cafeteria that was closed.

"Too bad," you say. "We could all do with a cup." You regret the inclusion, or exclusion, that the word "all" implies, but any qualification would make matters worse.

Encouraged, perhaps, by your comment, your daughter searches in her handbag. What she brings out is her mobile phone.

118

"You can't use that here," you tell her. "There are signs everywhere. You'll have to go outside."

"I'd like to take his picture," she says. "Can I, Mum?"

A picture, here? You shake your head. This is not how she will want to remember him. Nor would your husband want her to, of that you are sure. To your surprise, she doesn't argue but puts the phone away.

A little before five o'clock, you sense that there is a slight change in your husband's breathing. At first you can't determine what that change is – what little sound he makes has not altered at all – but then you realize that the pause between one breath and the next is longer than it was. You grow tense waiting, so intent on listening that you notice nothing else. This could go on forever, you think, fully aware that each breath could in fact be the last. This one. This one. You count the seconds between breaths. You slow the count down as if that would help keep him alive. One more. One more. And then, although there is no final spasm, no desperate last gasping for air, it is obvious that it is over. There is no sound.

A numbness comes over you. You feel shut off from everything around you, from the room you are in, from your son and daughter, but saying that is wrong: you do not feel. You look at the hand you are holding, but there is no one, no one, nothing, there. The truth leaps at you: you will never feel again.

Then someone must have fetched a nurse; it may well have been you. The tubes are gone. There is a doctor in the room – there are procedures that have to be followed.

"You'll want a little time alone with him," the doctor says. "Do you want me to close his eyes?"

"No," you say, "I'll do it."

But even as you do, as you move your hand slowly, gently, over your husband's forehead, past his eyes, and softly touch his lips with the inside of your thumb, you know that the picture you will carry with you, the one that will appear superimposed on every memory – when you glance at the chair that used to be his, or across the table where he used to sit, or at his side of the bed as you pull back the covers – what you will see will be what your eyes, your mind, have focused on all night, his head against the pillow, his face divided by the tubes, his eyes unblinking, staring blindly, seeing nothing. Nothing. That is what will remain with you.

You straighten the sheet across his chest.

"There," you say. "There."

But if the words really leave your lips, you are the only one who hears them. No one else.

Love

"My love," he told her, "knows no bounds."

"That's nice."

"It's Shakespeare, I think. Or Yeats."

"Yes," she said. "Would you like another potato?"

"It wouldn't be Lawrence, now, would it?"

"T. E.?"

"No. D. H."

"I doubt it. More meat?"

"What?"

"More meat? If not, I'll keep it for tomorrow."

"Yes. I may have heard it at school. We had this extraordinary teacher."

"Tilley."

"No, the other one. Stevens."

"It's amazing how some things stick."

"Isn't it! 'My love knows no bounds.' I think I'll have another potato. You want one?"

In the Year of the Summer of Love
(Elsewhere)

For Ray Davies, storyteller

They are young. They are unemployed. The latter is by choice. So much had been wrong at work. They had complained, but nobody listened and in the end they both simply handed in their notice. They never meant to leave, but when all they got from the office was a note of regret, insincere, no doubt, there was no alternative. There was no room for compromise. They had burned their bridges.

"They'll change their mind," Derek had said. "They'll send for us. We should leave a forwarding address."

This was the first time he had spoken of the future in terms of "we". They were not a couple, even though they had been spending a lot of time in each other's company. Did this mean they were leaving together?

"We don't have one," Cathy had pointed out, accepting the pronoun.

And that was true. When you leave a residential post, you end up homeless as well.

They are homeless.

"Try Brighton," someone suggested. "No one goes there in the winter, so it should be easy to find somewhere to live."

That seemed good advice. When the day came, they were late in starting. Having no plans, no goal beyond their destination, they had lingered over the meal in the staff dining room, unwilling to take the first step, and so the early January sun is about to set as they come out of the station and walk towards the centre of a town which is new to them. That may be a bad choice – accommodation will be cheaper further out. But for now they only want something temporary – it is too late in the day for anything else. They carry their luggage. It slows them down, but they assume that they will need cases to appear respectable – although a case and a holdall each may be overdoing it. They do not talk. Derek is the one who sets the pace; Cathy follows, doing her best not to slow him down. They have to rest now and then.

At an intersection they turn left, still some distance from the waterfront, as if by agreement, noting here and there signs that mean nothing to them: The Lanes, Kemp Town, and in the opposite direction, Hove. They trudge on, but have to pause more and more often. Then, down a side street, they see the kind of sign they have been hoping for: Holiday flatlets. Derek looks at Cathy. She nods.

"What do I say?" he asks.

"You want me to do it?"

"No, I will."

He is the man. He will be nineteen this year.

As it turns out, this is not something that he has to prove. Accepting what they are offered sight unseen, and paying in advance for the week it might take them to find something more permanent, they are given a key and instructions and make their way upstairs to look the place over: a large room with a gas fire and cooker, a double bed, two armchairs, a table and various odds and ends. The toilet and bathroom are down the hall. They leave their cases and go out to buy food, so Cathy can fix supper. Also they will need sixpences for the meter. Once they have found their way back, they eat in silence, mostly. Derek makes fun of the weight of the mugs, which, instead of a trademark, bear the name Hercules, but Cathy does not seem to see the joke. While she does the dishes, he worries about the double bed. What will come next? Will they have sex? The Durex he keeps in his wallet has been there so long that it has left a tell-tale imprint. What if it breaks? Too bad only married women can be on the pill. Will she want him to say that he loves her? Cross my heart? He lifts the mug to finish his tea and takes it over to the sink.

"I think we should make it an early night."

Cathy agrees. Then, as they undress, partially, back to back, before they take turns to go to the bathroom, she says: "I've got the curse." She does not know why – it is not something she had planned – but at least it should put off what might otherwise seem inevitable. At the same time, it is of course a promise of sorts: if I didn't... It was dumb of her.

It takes him a few seconds to catch on and a few more to respond, giving her a slight nod, forgetting perhaps that she has her back to him. He feels something like relief. When they get into bed, it is without touching, both equally careful to avoid slipping into the dip in the middle.

Rock Gardens, the name of the street, is a misnomer, they see in the morning, at least this time of year – last night, in the dark, it could have been called almost anything without inviting comment. Now, in its newness, everything does, and so they note the shops they did not see the night before, the bank where they might have to open an account, the dry cleaners. They have their work cut out for them, they tell each other; that is what happens when you are unemployed. They have to find somewhere to stay; they have to find a job. The last four weeks' wages are all they have; nor do they qualify for unemployment benefit, they have been told, not having paid enough contributions.

They do a lot of walking. This is both to get to know their way around and to follow up the handwritten ads in shop windows. There are a number of furnished flats available. They call at two addresses in Hove, but what they are offered turns out to be more than they can afford. "Third time lucky," they say, and they are. The rent, five guineas a week, should be within their means if at least one of them finds a job soon and for that they will get two rooms on the second floor. The kitchen is half a floor down; the bathroom, one they will share with other tenants, on the first floor. The flat is at the top of Bloomsbury Place.

"We could form a group," Cathy jokes, but Derek does not get the reference.

"How could we?" he says. "Neither of us plays an instrument."

He must have the song by The Kinks in mind, Cathy decides, the one they heard all through December, both on the BBC and pirate radio stations, though Bloomsbury Place is not literally a dead-end street – there is a narrow, half-concealed exit into Kemp Town. Still, they *are* out of work without any money coming in.

That remains their situation for a few weeks. They still go for long walks, visiting other places whose names prove not quite accurate, like the Undercliff walk, or sit in the living room of their new flat with the gas fire off in order to save money, scouring *The Argus* for a job they can apply for. January would appear not to be a good month. Some sort of routine is established: Cathy does the cleaning on a Saturday, the laundry on a Monday, as her mother used to do, the latter in the kitchen sink. Derek takes the rubbish out at night. As yet, although they sleep together, they have not slept with each other. It is as if the curse Cathy invoked has become permanent. Perhaps, she thinks, this will change once they find a job, not really sure if she wants it to or not.

"Here's one for you, Cathy," says Derek. He has gone back to the ads in *The Argus* after marking the place where the football must be in the Spot the ball competition. Cathy knows he is wrong. If you could work out where the ball should be by looking at the players' hands, or feet, or eyes, or heads, there would be no competition. He should look for the *least* likely place. But this she does not say. "Basket making. At least until you find something better. They'll send you all the material you need, with instructions, and then collect the baskets and pay for them."

Cathy merely makes a face. There are times when the two years she has on him really tell.

But without letting her know, he sends for the material, substituting his own surname for hers – their landlady had expected them to be married, so married they are. Their post, if any, has to show that.

And Cathy in turn, without letting him know, starts asking around for a job when she goes food shopping, approaching people in shops and offices wherever there might be an opening.

She is the one who is lucky. Derek's letter results only in an alternative offer: while more than enough basket weavers have applied, there is a shortage of tie makers. But Cathy will not be sewing ties. The day he gets the letter, she comes bounding up the stairs.

"Derek, I've got a job!" she announces. She proudly produces a packet of butter, as if this is it. No more Echo margarine spread thin.

"How?"

"They must have liked my looks," she jokes.

"They?"

"He," she says. "The manager. I went to some of the cinemas. The ABC... was it the ABC? Anyway, I know where it is. They want an usherette."

"An usherette?"

"An usherette. They provide the uniform. And a torch."

She waits for the echo: *A torch?* But there is none.

"In the intermission I'll be the Fruit Parfait Girl," she says. "The tray's a bit heavy. Still, the more I sell, the lighter my work. That's what the manager said. He's got quite a sense of humour."

"Is that really better than the job we had?" Derek asks.

She stares at him. "What do you mean? It's money."

"And that's all that counts?"

"Of course not. But I'm not exactly prostituting myself."

The look he gives her tells her that she is.

"I don't see you bringing in any money," she says. She regrets her words as soon as they are out.

"I wouldn't be an usherette even if I could. But I'll find something."

"I know," she says. "I'm sorry, Derek. I didn't mean it."

But even if she didn't, her point is valid, as they both know – her pay will not be enough in the long run.

Is it having a job that makes her turn towards him that night? Or is it having criticized him for not having one? She does not know. The fact remains that once they are in bed, with the light off, she turns over and puts her arm around him – he is lying on his side, with his back to her. She stays under the covers – the room is cold. At first he does not respond. Then he shifts a little, but not enough to face her.

"You want to?" he asks, so quietly that she can only just make out the words.

He must have felt her nod.

"You sure?"

"Yes."

"I need to get my wallet," he says, sitting up.

"Your what?" She is confused or else she would be angry. But then, as he swings his legs over the side and

127

takes two steps to get to the chair where his jacket is, she understands: it is neither a bad joke, nor an insult. "Oh." By that time he is back in the bed, facing her.

They have never given each other more than a hug before and when they did, that was standing up; now, lying on their side, holding each other, they have only one arm free. For him, since they are both right-handed, it is the wrong one. They touch awkwardly. They kiss equally awkwardly, she lightly, he with more force. Gradually their bodies begin to respond, his more than hers. He sits up and tears open the packet that he took from his wallet. When he is ready, he comes to her. "Wait," she says. "Wait. I'm not—" but he is pushing at her, hurting her. She adjusts her position and guides him and then it does not hurt and very soon he stops pushing and rolls over on his back.

She pulls down her nightdress. It takes her a while to go to sleep.

Last night was a mistake, Derek tells himself – he should not have let it happen. He goes to the bathroom and flushes down the condom. Too late he realizes that this is also a mistake: he should have made sure first that it was not broken. At least he had not lied and said he loved her.

Cathy is not in the living room; she must have gone out. He picks up yesterday's *Argus* and looks through the ads again. There is nothing he can apply for; the few jobs that are advertised all call for qualifications that he does not have. He has no education – he only did a few months at art college. He has no driving licence. Perhaps he should put in an ad himself. *Good-for-nothing inexperienced eighteen-year-old male looking for work in Brighton and its environs.* Strike the word male, he thinks.

She must have been disappointed. He knows he would do better without foreplay – it gets him too excited – but

128

girls expect it, don't they? He should have pretended he was asleep. Now she is probably pregnant and there is nothing they can do about it.

Do you have to pay a fee to get married?

He goes down to the kitchen, fills the kettle and puts some toast on. As he is buttering it – butter! – he hears Cathy on the stairs. He opens the door.

"I'm making toast. Do you want some?"

"Please," she says. "It's cold out." She takes off her coat and sits down at the kitchen table. It is cold in the kitchen too. "We need to talk, Derek," she says. "Last night was a mistake."

"I know. Let's just forget it happened, right? Tea?"

"You have to get a job," she says.

He nods even though he cannot see the connection. "I will, Cathy." He pours her tea.

"I mean it. We can't get by on what I'll be getting."

"I'll get a job."

"You could ask at the supermarkets."

"They only want women."

"Not in the store rooms."

"OK, I'll ask," he says.

"Today."

"OK," he says. "Do you want marmalade?"

"Or at the hospitals. There's one up the road."

"Me a nurse?" he says. "No way."

"You need training for that. But you could be a porter. Thanks."

"I'll ask."

"Or do maintenance or something. You can wire a plug, can't you? Fix a toilet that's running?"

"I've seen my dad do it."

"Cleaning, then. There's always a need for cleaners. Just to see us through. Until you find something better."

"OK."

"Today, Derek? Please?"

"OK," he says. "I will."

He goes to get dressed. He leaves his cup on the table. She takes hers into the living room.

After Derek has gone out, Cathy wonders if he will do more than just wander the streets. She regrets that she did not bring up the question that was really on her mind, the one she had been turning over when she was out walking but had no answer for. Why are they together at all? What kind of relationship does he want? What does she want? His gesture, offering her tea and toast, had surprised her; he had hardly set foot in the kitchen before, except to eat the meals she prepared. Does this mean that he will now be more considerate? Or was he just apologizing for last night?

Not that he needed to. The initial mistake had been hers; what followed was probably unavoidable. She has heard others speak of similar experiences. "Men," her mother would have sighed, if they had ever talked about sex. "Men."

It is not Monday, but she decides to do the laundry anyway – Monday she will be at work. Her hours will include weekends now and then, the manager told her, but she will have other days off in lieu. And the mornings will be her own; she will be able to do her housework more or less the way she does it now.

She washes out Derek's shirts, socks and underwear as well as her own things and hangs them out to dry on the line that runs from the kitchen window across the shaft to the building next door. It does not take long, so she decides to do the sheets and pillowcases they had had to buy – the furnished flat did not include towels and sheets. She puts them on to boil in a big pot. They will hardly be dry by evening. She will have to remember to bring them in and spread them out over some chairs in front of the fire.

Derek has not returned by the time she is finished. When he does, mid-afternoon, he shakes his head. He has had no luck.

He remains out of luck. Each morning Cathy waves him off, figuratively, not to set eyes on him again until he comes to meet her at the cinema and walk her home; she has asked him to. It is not that she is afraid, not really; still, she does not know if the streets are safe at night. They rarely see each other except on her day off, but even then he is out most of the time. When he comes home, she cooks for the two of them; at other times he fixes his own meals. She does the cleaning and the laundry and she shops for groceries; he tends to forget. She makes the sandwiches she takes to work.

Derek tells her of some of the places he has tried but gives her no detailed account. "You wouldn't happen to have a job for me, would you?" is the question he asks and it is always met with a shake of the head. Sometimes he is told to come back after Easter when things should pick up; there is nothing this time of year. Easter is a long way off. He tells her, too, that he checks the situations vacant column in the national papers at the library most every day; not all ads for local jobs even will be in *The Argus*. He does not tell her that he actually spends more time reading magazines than flicking through newspapers. Nor does he tell her of the record shop he has found, where the man behind the counter seems to enjoy his company as long as the owner is not in, talking of this and that and playing music Derek has not heard before. When he has been in and out almost every day for three weeks, to reciprocate, he

131

buys the single by The Kinks that has been on the radio a lot; a single is about all he can afford. The man puts it on; it is the first time Derek hears the B-side, *Big Black Smoke*. Then he asks for a job.

"You wouldn't be needing an assistant by any chance?"

But that is what the man is himself.

"You'd be better off in London," he says. He nods at the record. "All you need is a girlfriend to pay the rent. Brighton's dead in the winter."

"You're not kidding," says Derek. He turns up his collar. "Be seeing you."

But he knows he won't. He makes his decision then and there. He should never have set foot in Brighton.

Cathy is laughing and chatting with the other women as they get into their street clothes after work. She has just told them about the old man who wanted a fruit parfait. "Could you put it in my left hand, love," he had said, not quite facing her, "and then give me the spoon. I'm blind." Now, what was a blind man doing at the cinema?

"He probably came in to keep warm," Helen suggests. "Heating's expensive."

Pensioners pay less in the afternoon, Cathy knows.

"At least he doesn't have to see Omar Sharif looking all teary-eyed," says Brenda, who is appalled at the long run of what she considers trash – she is very particular about her likes and dislikes. She has taken to Cathy; Cathy is going to her place for tea the day after tomorrow, when they both have some time off.

"See you," Cathy calls out as she leaves to meet Derek.

But Derek is not there. She was going to tell him too of the incident – it has been a long time since they had a good laugh together – but it will have to wait. He might have fallen asleep on the sofa. If so, it does not really matter; she

132

is familiar with the streets by now and can take care of herself.

And this is, of course, what she will have to do: when she gets home and opens the door to the living room, what she finds is not Derek but some kind of present, gift-wrapped, propped up on the table. Nor is he in the bedroom, where she sees only what is missing: the clothes that should have been lying around; the suitcase and holdall that should have been under the bed; the shirts, trousers and underwear that should have been in the wardrobe and drawers. She does not even bother to go down to the kitchen. He is gone.

There is a note with the present. "This isn't working," it reads. He has not signed it. She removes the wrapping paper and there is *Dead End Street* by The Kinks. Since she has no record player, she cannot put it on. She is curious about the flip side.

Poor Derek – this is so childlike, leaving her a present, as if that would make a difference. Did he feel that he owed her something? If so, why a record? Was it cheaper than chocolates? Or – she is suddenly suspicious – is it meant as a gibe: you can keep your dead-end street – I'm out of here? But Derek has never been spiteful, has he? She does not know what to think.

It is late but she puts on the kettle anyway. She is not in shock, exactly – or maybe she is: you don't expect the person you are living with to just take off without a word of warning. At the same time, she discovers, she feels something like relief – the last few weeks especially have been frustrating. She has some thinking to do. It is clear that she cannot stay in the flat, at least not if she goes on working at the cinema. She will have to find cheaper lodgings as soon as possible. Brenda might know of a place. It is a good thing she is seeing her on Thursday.

Perhaps this whole business will bring her period on –
she is now more than a week overdue.

She takes her empty cup to the kitchen to rinse it out
and notices a plate standing on the side. Derek must have
eaten before he left. By the looks of it he had fried eggs on
toast; he never was much of a cook. She has to really scrub
the plate and cutlery to remove the egg. This time of night
the water is not very hot, after people have had their baths.

When she is done, she gets into her nightdress without
bothering to wash, then decides to sleep on the right side of
the bed from now on, which would have been her natural
choice. She pulls the cover up to her chin to keep warm – the
bedroom is colder than ever. She will not be here for long,
though. Another week or two at the outside and then… She
does not know what *then* will entail, but right now it does not
matter. She is young. She has a job. She has a place to stay.
Everything will work out for the best somehow.

Derek is equally confident, walking the streets not of
London but of East Croydon, which had meant a cheaper
fare – not a tourist town this time, but a place in its own
right. His luggage is at the station. He will pick it up
tomorrow, after he has got a job and found somewhere to
live. He anticipates no problems. He is young. He can take
care of himself. He is a man.

And in a little more than eight months, as if to prove it,
he will be a father. Of course, this he may never get to
know.

No Bear

Lynn shakes her head. "Not that I envy him."

"Your father?"

"Well, him neither. But it was my brother I was talking about. Hugh."

"So you were."

"Things have always fallen into his lap."

"I know what you mean."

Both raise their glasses, regarding the half-empty room – Mondays are quiet in this part of town. Colleagues rather than friends, they have reached the stage where they begin to exchange confidences.

"I hadn't heard from him for ages. Then he sent me this photo."

"Of himself?"

"That would have made more sense. No. His son had given him some sort of fancy camera."

"His son? You didn't tell me he had a son. How old is he?"

"What difference does it make? Anyway, the camera had an infrared sensor, to take pictures in the dark. He fixed it up outside his weekend place in North Carolina."

A gesture from Sue indicates that this is going too fast.

"Your brother has a house in the States?"

"Two. He moved there... oh, years ago. Best place to get ahead, he claimed. Not like here."

"What does he do?"

"Something related to finance. He never said. I never asked. I bet you can't guess what the picture showed."

"Was this by a lake?"

"No. Why?"

"I just wondered."

"The cabin's on a mountainside. He goes there to relax."

There is a long pause. The people at the table next to theirs get up to leave. Chairs scrape against the floor. They both watch them.

"Indians?" Sue suggests.

"No."

A short pause.

"Well, what?"

"A bear."

"He sent you a picture of a bear?"

"He did."

"I don't know what to say."

"He was boasting, of course. 'See what looked in on us the other night? Beat that if you can!' "

"Yes."

"I haven't even got a son."

"No."

"And if I did, I'm bloody sure he wouldn't buy me a camera."

"Well…"

"Why should he?"

"No, I suppose not."

"All right, he might. But then, if I were to rig it up outside my door, what could possibly set it off? You know my area."

"I do. No bear."

"No bear. Probably a Peeping Tom. Or a flasher."

"Yes."

They hear the call for last orders. Staring vacantly in front of them, they finish off what is in their glasses.

"Shall we have another one?"

"I don't mind if I do."

"It's so unfair. If I were a man, life would be so different."

"You're right there."

136

They shake their heads in unison.

No bear.

They part outside and make for the nearest bus stop –
neither of them can afford a taxi. Lynn's is round the corner
– she was the one who proposed that they meet at The
Crown. When her bus arrives, it is as empty as the pub. She
slumps down in a seat, casting a casual glance out of the
window. There are few lights and what she sees, bumping
along, is her own reflection. Her brother is on her mind. She
raises a hand to fluff up her hair but stops in mid-air,
startled. With its nose flat against the window, not two feet
away, is the head of a bear. She blinks. It is still there.

And then it is gone, its place taken by a man wearing an
anorak with a fur-lined hood.

Not quite recovered, she looks across the aisle. "I took
you for a bear," she says.

But the man is one seat up and doesn't respond.

"Your reflection in the window," she explains. "The
fur."

Now he catches on. "It's fake," he points out. "Not bear."

"Not bear."

She regrets having addressed him. He could get the
wrong idea. To forestall that, she concentrates on the
window. The man's head remains in view, hooded, off
centre, not quite in focus, like the bear in the photo her
brother sent.

He had never been much of a photographer. An only
child until she came along, he had been spoiled all his life,
showered with expensive gifts he didn't need and didn't
know how to handle. Before her appears the cassette
recorder that he ruined within weeks. Beside it is the
camera whose many settings had him baffled –
photography, in those days, was a craft. In addition to his

technical ineptitude, his timing was off, as she learned to her dismay. Again and again his flashcubes caught a face she never made – or, if she did, made only for that sixtieth of a second when he chose to press the trigger. Naturally he delighted in the distortions that followed, her mouth drooping or twisted out of shape; eyes squint, crossed, bulging; nose twitching, exploding in a sneeze. Those were the shots he kept; if there were others, he hid them from sight. She heard him in his room, laughing with his mates, and easily figured out why. The memory hurts.

Of course, in this instance he hadn't actually held the camera. Even so, it could have been aimed more directly at the spot where the bear had activated it. It was all a matter of calculation – and calculation used to be his forte.

"You don't want any pudding, do you?" he might say. "You left half your potatoes."

Her mum, on her way to the kitchen, would stop in mid-stride. "Is that true?" she would ask.

And so he would get Lynn's share of whatever was for dessert.

Occasionally he would admit to having made a mistake. One he kept coming back to was not studying Chinese – not that it was a language offered at his school, but there were ways and means, he said; yes, ways and means. And he would nod to indicate the ease with which the rules could be bent if you were in the know. Someone had tricked him into doing French. He had dropped the subject at an early stage, but being inventive when it came to teasing, found some use for it all the same, taunting Lynn with what little he knew, as if she were to blame. "Comprehensive school," he might snort. "That's for those who *comprennent pas rien*. You comprehend? *Pas rien*."

Eleven at the time, she knew better than to ask what the phrase meant.

The bus pulls up abruptly at a stop, but no one boards it. She catches a glimpse of a dark figure backing away. Like her brother, he must have made a mistake, having had a different destination in mind – unless, like her, he had spotted the bear. She chokes back a giggle, which results in a cough. Embarrassed, she brings out her handkerchief and wipes her mouth and nose, but a quick look behind her satisfies her that no one noticed her moment of exuberance. The driver sets the bus in motion. His mumbled curse, if that is what it is, is drowned out by the noise from the engine as he shifts to a higher gear.

So her brother never got to do Chinese – which would have left him part ruler of the world – but what of it? Unlike her, he got to go to grammar school, then on to university and cushy jobs, and now he lives in what for him, and no doubt for the bear, must be a land of milk and honey.

Hold it, she tells herself. Honey, indeed, but milk? Do bears care for milk once they have left the cub stage?

She ponders the question, but is side-tracked, landing on the doorstep of her childhood home, where the milkman placed their bottles in the early morning. Who brought them inside? It wasn't her brother, that much she knows. Mornings found him sound asleep. Nor, being a boy, did he have any other chores, whereas she, four years his junior, was expected to help in countless ways, setting and clearing the table, doing the dishes, lending a hand with cleaning, shopping and what not, from an early age.

She meets the driver's eyes in the rear-view mirror. Is he as frustrated with his role as she had been – as she is, even today, over what happened as she grew up? His swearing may have been an indication that this is so. At the same time, his job must introduce few new hassles. For her, because she was a girl, duties were added all the time; her brother, male and hence privileged, had nothing to contend with but his homework. While he pored over his books, or pretended to, it fell to her lot to clean his shoes, to press the trousers of his school uniform.

Cinderella, she thinks, minus the mice.

At least the latter task came to an end the day she produced a conspicuous burn mark halfway up the leg. She pictures herself staring at the area that stood out even in the poorly lit corner of the kitchen where she did her work. She had turned the iron over to check the underside. She hadn't touched it, which was just as well. To this day she can't tell if what happened was the result of carelessness or anger – she was thirteen at the time. She hopes it was deliberate. She hopes she simply pretended to herself that it came about by accident. In any case, though her pocket money was stopped for weeks, she never lost any sleep over it. Revenge, albeit unintentional, can be sweet.

The bus is approaching her neighbourhood; it has stopped only once to let people off. The man across the aisle is still there. She takes a peek at him in an attempt to note the state of his trousers, but the back of the empty seat beside him hides them from view. These days, of course, few men wear trousers that need pressing, unless they work in banks or posh offices. The anorak suggests that neither is the case.

And then, her eyes fixed on the fur-lined hood, it comes to her in a flash: what she should do is return her brother's favour – give him a quid pro quo, as those who have been to university might put it. Dearest Hugh.

Quietly, she snaps her handbag open, brings out her mobile phone. After checking her appearance in the window and patting her hair into shape, she gets to her feet. In two steps she has reached the man's seat. She holds up her phone.

"I wonder…" she says.

His eyes shift from the phone to her face.

"Yes?"

"A picture. Would you mind?"

"You want me to take your picture?"

"No, no," she explains, "I'll take it. Of the two of us. May I?"

He is confused.

"What for? I'm nobody."

"Oh, but you're not." How persuade him? "It's for my brother," she offers.

It doesn't work.

"He lives in the U.S. We hardly ever see each other." Plead, she instructs herself. "It's been years since we met."

"That's sad."

The man appears moved. Or is he merely being polite?

"It won't take a second."

"All right."

He puts up his hands to flip back the hood of his anorak, but she interrupts him. "No, no, leave it as it was." Quickly she slides in beside him. With the phone raised above eye level, she makes sure she's not blocking the lens. She leans closer and produces a grin. A light touch, and she is done. She checks the result, allowing the man a quick glance. That should do. It is on a par with those her brother took of her as a child.

They are approaching her stop. She reaches for the button, puts the phone away. "You've been very kind," she says.

His eyes are a warm brown.

"I had a younger sister," he tells her. "We were close."

The driver slows down, comes to a halt. With a smile less lopsided than in her pose, she curtseys her way off the bus.

"My bear," she will announce when she mails the photo

to her brother, "captured at 11:37 on a Monday night. A rare sight in this region."

She pauses in her thoughts. "He had a sister," she could add, "who meant a lot to him. I reminded him of her." Should she elaborate, invent? He supported her through school. O levels. A levels. About to enter university, she caught a rare disease and died. Life can be so cruel.

No, she decides. She will send the photo, with nothing but the briefest caption. That will do.

As the bus passes her, she notes that the man in the anorak is heading for the exit. He must live in the area. She quickens her pace almost inadvertently, but then changes her mind. She doesn't know him. If he did have a sister, it is no guarantee that he would treat her like one – whatever that would mean. She crosses the road to where the streetlights are. Two minutes, and she will be home. No bears, thank you. Don't put yourself at risk. You are much better off without one.

Aren't you?

Only Sometimes

He moves closer. What he sees is another landscape, barren, with little in it other than ice, a landscape in which to lose oneself. The fog has cancelled out details. In the foreground are a few frozen reeds. There is no horizon.

"When did you paint this?" he asks.

"About a year ago."

"We shouldn't have broken up."

"Everything's not about you, Gary."

"And this?" He walks over to the next canvas.

Even though the scene is an indoor view, the painting is twice the size of the landscape – why place them side by side? It shows the left half of a double bed, the bedclothes thrown back, the pillow bunched up, the sheet wrinkled. On the floor lies an open book. A dark shadow falls across the part of the bed that is visible.

"Me?" he asks.

She shrugs.

Now he sees the title: "Man." There is a red dot on the label. So four have been sold already. That is impressive. She must be making quite some money.

A woman their age wants to talk to Louise and the glass of wine she is holding indicates that she will be a while. Of course, that is what a *vernissage* is for. He strolls past the last few canvases, a tousled cat and an equally tousled dog, and then heads for the exit. He can always call her.

Outside it is already dark and yet this is only a hint of what is coming – he has a whole long winter ahead of him. He wraps the scarf around him, turns up the collar of his jacket and heads for his favourite haunt in the Haymarket area, One Step Up. It is a bit early, but he doesn't feel like going home. Apparently he isn't the only one. Inside, he catches sight of Ian at one of the tables. He gets himself a beer and goes over to him.

"Hi," he says, as he pulls out a chair. He sits down, gestures with his bottle. "Cheers."

"Mind if I join you?" says Ian.

"No, not at all. I'm not expecting anyone. Make yourself at home."

"Sorry." Gary has known Ian since they studied business law together but still can't tell for sure when he is joking. "You looked like you could do with some company. Isn't Anne back?"

Anne isn't back. She may have left for good this time, but Ian has thought so before.

"And you?" he asks in turn. "This is early for you."

"I've been to a *vernissage*. I'm on my way home."

"Since when did you take an interest in paintings? Wait. Don't tell me. Some girl, right?"

"Louise."

Ian shakes his head. "Come on, Gary. How long is it since you split up? Two years? Three? Forget about her." He stops. "Sorry. Did she send you an invite?"

"An invite? No."

"So you were gate-crashing."

"Well, we were close."

Ian makes a face.

"She misses me. It's obvious when you look at her paintings. I'm there. You should see her portraits. There are women longing for contact. There are pets. Cats and dogs with enormous pupils. She used to do abstracts."

"So? Forget about her. There's plenty of fish in the sea." Ian looks around, but the place is almost empty. "Anyway, it's time you moved on."

But Gary can't forget about her. The next morning, Louise is still on his mind, even though Amy is the one who spent the night with him. This isn't something he remembers

144

initially. It is only when he hears sounds from the kitchen that he vaguely recollects that she showed up at the pub. I hope she has enough sense to leave, he thinks. It must be late. He closes his eyes to shut out the light. All he wants to do is go back to sleep.

"Ah, you're awake." The voice comes from the doorway. "You don't want any coffee, do you?"

His grunt can mean only one thing.

"Then I'll be on my way. Don't forget to lock the door. I'll be seeing you."

The evening had clearly not been a success. Now Amy will be offended forever. Louise, he thinks. Louise. Louise would never... His head is pounding and his thoughts get stuck; he can't remember what it is Louise would never do. Louise would never... Louise... Louise... The name hits him again and again.

A few hours later he is still quite shaky but gets up anyway, showers and finds some yoghurt in the fridge. He eats it straight from the carton. This is one of the advantages of being single: it cuts down on the washing-up. And at that thought he remembers what Louise would never have done: she would not have come home with him in that state. With her, if he wanted company, he had to stay reasonably sober. In fact, letting go was the last thing she herself would do, even when she was painting. It is true she could use a palette knife, or her fingers, instead of a brush when she was working with oils, but that was just to achieve a different structure. It had nothing to do with feelings. She would never lose control.

At least this is what he'd assumed – he'd never actually seen her paint. He could only judge by the result.

"When I shut the door, I want to be on my own." That was one of the rules she established when she moved in.

At first he hadn't taken her seriously – painting wasn't exactly a secret vice. In the early days, he could open the door

145

to the room they'd set aside for her just to offer her a cup of coffee, but he soon learned not to. Knocking on the door was equally wrong. He wasn't just superfluous; he was a nuisance.

Not that it had bothered him. He hadn't been all that curious about her paintings. If she wanted to paint, that was fine with him. He used to collect stamps as a child. He'd doubted that she would ever make it as an artist, but then she didn't need to. Working as a supply teacher brought in enough cash. Before she moved in with him, it must have been a bit harder though.

Now things have picked up, it seems.

Gary switches on his PC and googles "Louise Katell". He hasn't done this for a while, but the only new entry seems to be an interview. "Artist in the making" is the title, a phrase that doesn't exactly promise wonders, but still – in a way he is impressed.

She must have been "in the making" even when they met, he realizes, but that wasn't something he'd been aware of then. The whole thing had been so accidental. He'd arranged to go to the pictures with Amy, but she'd called when he was waiting in the foyer. Something had come up. Since he was there anyway, he'd decided to see the film on his own. He'd bought a ticket, had it checked and hurried on down a poorly lit corridor. He'd been a bit late, but the film hadn't started – the trailers were just coming on when he opened the door. He'd assumed they had delayed the start because there was only one other person in the audience. He'd chosen a seat a few rows back from her.

Much later Anne had asked how they'd met, he and Louise – this was when they'd gone out together, the four of them.

"At the cinema," Louise had said. "At least that's where we first saw each other. We were the only people in town who knew to appreciate Mike Leigh. A fantastic film."

146

Gary had never told her the reason he was there. The truth was that he'd entered the wrong auditorium. It had taken a while before he'd understood what had happened. In fact, with all the ads and trailers – and the opening of the film itself, which he'd taken to be another trailer since it wasn't at all what he'd expected – he must have missed a full fifteen minutes of the action film he and Amy had meant to see, which was due to start earlier. So he'd decided to stay put. How could he have known that this was a film with no action whatsoever? Nothing happened. To his surprise he'd heard Louise laugh now and then.

"I stayed on to check the credits, but Gary left as soon as the film was over. And then I ran into him the next day at the station. 'Weren't you the one at the cinema yesterday?' he asked. So we went and had coffee. You can't fight against destiny."

Gary knew then, as he knows now, that the bit about destiny had been a joke. Louise isn't a believer in destiny. At the same time it was important to her that they'd been the only ones who had seen the film. Even though she didn't use that word, she implied that they must be twin souls. He should have told her the truth, of course, but then she would no doubt have lost interest. How honest should you be in a relationship? Not too honest, in his view. Ian had heard Gary's version but hadn't let on. Luckily Louise hadn't noticed how little he'd had to contribute when they discussed the film, even though that was practically the only topic of conversation. It was almost as if they'd seen different films. After that he'd come up with excuses to avoid having to go to the pictures with her. They had so many other things in common.

So what had gone wrong? It isn't the first time Gary asks himself that question, but he has no more of an answer now than before. In the beginning they mostly saw each other in company – rarely alone. Then there was a period when they

147

kept to themselves. They had sex, of course, but not as much as he'd anticipated. After that they started going out again, spending two or three nights a week together, either at his place or hers – more often hers. It worked quite well.

That makes him wonder why they decided to live together. Whose idea was that? It wasn't really a move either of them could have taken for granted. They were both used to an independent life. He doubts that it could have been Louise's suggestion and it definitely wasn't his. His first and only lasting relationship before Louise came to an abrupt end when his girlfriend started to make plans for the future.

He calls Ian.

"Is Anne back?" he asks. It isn't what he meant to say – why remind him?

Anne isn't back. Gary changes the subject.

"There's something I'd like to talk to you about," he says.

"OK."

"Can we meet over a beer?"

But Ian doesn't feel like going out. It's Sunday. They both have to get up early.

"Is it about Amy?" he asks.

"Amy? Why would it be about Amy?"

"She might have said something."

"About what?"

"How would I know? It was just a thought."

"No. It's about Louise."

And Ian agrees to meet him.

"Around eight?" Gary suggests. He needs to take another shower and also has to get something to eat – not just yoghurt.

Groundhog Day, he thinks as he opens the door to One Step Up – it feels as if he has rewound the tape twenty-four hours. But that is what it is like when you've been living in the same place for a while – more than ten years now. Everything becomes routine. The same pubs. The same tables. The same beer. Perhaps he should move.

This time, though, Ian isn't there. In actual fact it takes so long before he turns up that Gary is beginning to wonder if he has changed his mind. He was definitely not enthusiastic, for some reason. Gary has got used to having Ian around whenever he needs him.

The reason he is late, it turns out, is that Anne called just as he arrived at the pub. He wanted to finish talking to her before going inside.

"She'll be here tomorrow," he says, "so I have to do some cleaning. I can't stay long."

"I was wondering why Louise moved in with me," Gary blurts out.

"So you could be together, of course." Ian looks surprised. "Now, what did you want to talk to me about? As I said, I'm in a bit of a hurry." He takes a swig of his beer.

"That's it."

"Why she moved in with you?"

"Yes. We saw each other almost every day as it was."

Ian shrugs.

"What difference does it make? You tried it out. It worked for a while and then it didn't. You split up. That's what happens. Why go on about it?"

"I'm not going on about it. I'm just trying to understand."

"OK. You decided to live together because it's easier. It saves time. It saves money. No trips back and forth. No clothes to haul around. No food in the fridge that goes off."

"All very practical."

"Isn't that enough? But why ask me? Don't you know yourself?"

149

"I don't remember. Presumably one of us suggested it, but it wasn't me. And I'm pretty sure it wasn't Louise either."

"The suggestion came from Anne," says Ian. It sounds as if it is so self-evident that it doesn't even have to be stated. "We'd just got our flat and she was as pleased as could be. But don't blame her. It was your decision. You didn't have to be persuaded. If I remember correctly we were having an evening out and you sat jotting down figures on a serviette to see how much rent money each of you would save. Just what one would expect from someone who works to minimize company expenditure."

"Senior Claims Adjuster. We've been given new titles – a no-cost promotion strategy, to widen the meaning of that term. Actually, it was my brainchild. But to get back to Louise, I'm not trying to blame anyone. I just wonder what went wrong."

"You make it sound as if it all happened as soon as Louise moved in. I thought things were fine to start with. I don't know what happened later. Sleeping with Amy can't have helped."

Is this what friends are for? Two fingers on the Bible, and all that? Gary makes a face. "Don't remind me," he says. "But Louise never found out."

"They always do. That's why Anne left again."

"Because…?"

"Yes."

Is he proud or embarrassed? It is impossible to tell. Gary is almost envious. He has no one to be unfaithful towards.

"Who was it?"

"It doesn't matter."

Louise? Is that why Ian keeps telling him to forget about her? It must be someone he knows, otherwise Ian wouldn't refuse to answer. But would Louise be interested in Ian?

150

Gary decides to ask even if he doesn't really expect an answer.

"Louise?"

Ian gives him an empty look and shakes his head. "Always Louise. I'm sorry to disappoint you." He pushes his chair back. "Now I have to be off. I don't want Anne to come walking in before I've cleaned up. Cheers."

And he leaves.

Gary stays. He isn't expecting anyone else to turn up, not on a Sunday night, but he might as well hang around here as at home.

What was it that hadn't worked? Everything had seemed fine at first, Ian had said, and that was true. When they argued it was generally about something trivial like cleaning or cooking. Shopping. Laundry, occasionally. And a lot of it had to do with the fact that he was more tolerant than her. A little dust here and there didn't bother him; actually, he never noticed. And if he did, he didn't think it mattered. The problem was that Louise was so pedantic. Why pull out the cooker and clean behind it? He hadn't in all the years he'd been living in the flat. The same with the front panel of the bathtub. If you had to lie down flat and press your cheek against the floor to even see the dust and the dried-in water stains, they couldn't do much harm, could they? Still, if that was how Louise wanted to spend her time, she was welcome to it. He did his part of what he thought needed doing.

The same when it came to preparing food. He was used to eating out now and then or else he'd pick up something that only needed heating. If Louise wanted to spend time cooking, fine. For him, that wasn't an option: he got home far too late. Louise complained of course, but what else could he do? It wasn't as if he didn't do his bit. And they didn't exactly fight. She grumbled and he let her.

151

And none of their quarrels had anything to do with Amy, as Ian thought. If Louise had had the least inkling, she would have told him in no uncertain terms.

Of course, there were times when things got a bit out of hand. Once he'd pointed out that she had more free time than him – which he shouldn't have done. She did *not* work half time, she said – painting was work, too. If she chose not to earn money, that was her business. She paid her share.

He had to agree. She was right.

But deep inside he knew that she was only partly right. And in the end, after he'd held his tongue any number of times, he couldn't do it any longer. It was a fact, he'd said, that no one stood over her with a whip when she kept herself busy with her paintings. She could take off whenever she wanted. She could sit down and watch TV. She could go for a walk. She could do as she pleased. There would be no consequences. And that was the difference between them. He couldn't. And it was the same with her teaching. If she couldn't take a class, somebody else would keep the kids occupied.

"So what I'm doing is of no importance?"

She'd seemed so calm that he'd thought she'd be open to his argument.

"In a way. It's possible that you'll be recognized one day, but the chances are pretty slim. There are so many others who are at least equally good. But it doesn't mean that you can't get something out of it yourself."

"And my *real* job? My teaching?"

The way she'd stressed the word should have put him on his guard, but didn't. "I suppose there's nothing wrong with it," he'd said. "But teaching kids to draw – you can't really compare it with maths, for instance."

"It's not just drawing that I do – art involves a lot more

than that. But regardless, why can't you compare it with maths?"

"It's not needed the same way, is it?"

"There are different kinds of needs," she'd said. "But I'm beginning to see that that idea is beyond you."

Not at all, he'd wanted to say. But when he tried to explain what he meant, they were still talking at cross purposes. She couldn't follow him. And shortly after that she'd left.

He goes over to the bar for another beer, even though he should be on his way home. If only Louise had been able to listen, it needn't have ended the way it did.

The local paper reviews films on Fridays and new records and computer games midweek, he knows, but exhibitions? Would there even be a day set aside for them? Gary checks the web version of the paper both Monday and Tuesday, but there is no review. This comes as no great surprise. One might think they would pick up on local talent, but it could be that Louise is too insignificant. And then he forgets to check until Ian calls. By then it is Friday afternoon.

"Did you see the review?" he asks. "Both Anne and Amy got curious. They're going there. I hope they don't run into each other."

He couldn't have been more explicit: it must have been Amy and not Louise that Ian had slept with. In a way Gary feels relieved, but at the same time he is annoyed. They never used to encroach on each other's territory. What's going on? Besides, Ian is obviously still seeing her. That isn't fair to him nor very smart. Anne is bound to be suspicious for a while.

Gary turns to his PC, goes to the opening page of the paper and types in Louise's name – he forgot to ask Ian when the review had appeared. He hits the return key. There

153

is one entry only, from yesterday. He clicks on the name of the article. There is a picture of one of Louise's landscapes beside the text. He chooses the print option to clear the page of advertising and other material and then reads the review, growing more and more irritated.

Scarred Lives

The unspoken in focus

By Carrie Edgars

The Eco Café Nov 23 – Dec 8

When a young artist has her first separate exhibition, especially if it is held in a modest venue, it often has the appearance of a retrospective. There is likely to be a mixture of early efforts and more mature work. Subjects and styles may vary a great deal. The artist will be trying things out, it seems, for good and for bad. This is not the case with Louise Katell. Hers is one of the most consistent shows I have seen in years. Katell knows what she wants and has chosen her exhibits with the utmost care.

At first sight such a statement may appear almost absurd. At the Eco Café, the range is wide: there are landscapes and interiors as well as portraits of both people and animals. But the seemingly disparate subjects have strong thematic links. Katell moves in the terrain of the exposed. The women who are portrayed – and there are no men to be seen

– are women who have been deprived of their identity. Their looks are empty. They have had their features distorted by the ideals of beauty in today's society and their reaction is one of apathy. In some instances they are not even present in the room. A canvas entitled "Man" shows the woman as a book torn open, its back cracked. Beside it is the empty landscape where she has had to find refuge. The title is superfluous, of course – one of few times when Katell makes use of an unnecessary pointer. Mostly we get to read the subtext on our own.

This is an exhibition that will affect most viewers profoundly. At the exit are three canvases of abused pets, but in these there is none of the submission so evident in the portraits of the women. Even though their skin is torn, their coats clotted with blood, their teeth and claws represent a real threat, as if that were the only possible answer to the situation they are in. I am deeply shaken as I leave.

How can anyone be so biased? Gary has no bone to pick with feminists, but this is going too far. Empty looks! Apathy! Threat! It is a good thing he has seen the exhibition himself or else he would have ended up with a very skewed impression of what it is about. He wonders how – what was her name? – how Edgars would view him. Well, actually he doesn't. He'd rather not know. No doubt she judges all men alike.

At least Louise is more nuanced. It's not about you – those were her words when he'd commented on one of the landscapes.

Mind you, at the same time the review is very positive. He glances through the text again and notes words like "consistent" and "utmost care". If he were in advertising, these are the words he would use as selling points. The opening and closing sentence of the final paragraph would also be very effective. He almost smiles to himself: he can't recall ever having read a review of an exhibition before and now he is behaving as if he were Louise's agent – if artists have agents. And she was the one who complained that he didn't understand her!

Suddenly he knows what he is going to do. He is going to see the exhibition again and buy one, perhaps even two of the canvases, two portraits probably – those women with a yearning look. They could turn into a profitable investment. If nothing else it will please Louise – she will no doubt find out who the buyer is. She might even come to see that she has misjudged him.

He prints the review, folds it and puts it in his pocket. Then he turns off the lights: it is almost five o'clock. He hums as he locks the door to his office. The Eco Café will be his first stop. After that there is a whole weekend to enjoy. He prefers not to put into words what that might entail. Sometimes surprising things happen.

The Sound of Patriarchy

Colin recognizes only two of his neighbours and has spoken
to neither – it is only a few weeks since he moved in. He
still feels temporary. Now, as he bumps into one of them on
the stairs, he does.

"They're for my little girl," he explains. "It's her
birthday."

"Five?" says the neighbour.

"Six. The wind took one."

"Helium?"

"I didn't ask."

"I always get one more, just in case. To be prepared for
the worst."

"That would take more than a balloon."

"True."

She seems about to add something but then just nods.
They part. As they do, Colin sees that he made a mistake.
The woman is not his neighbour. Never mind. There is no
harm in being friendly.

Outside the wind has picked up, but he holds the
balloons in a firm grip. It takes some manoeuvring to get
them on the bus, though. As he states his fare, puts the
money in the box and picks up his ticket, the driver looks
at him. Bringing balloons may not have been a good idea.
Prams, dirty dogs – he has heard there are restrictions.

"They're for my little girl," he says. This time it is an
apology. "It's her birthday."

"Helium?" asks the driver.

Would that be bad?

"I don't think so. Why?"

The driver shrugs his shoulders; he does not care. Colin
moves to an empty seat. The balloons surround him. They
are like clouds, he thinks, clouds or a halo.

157

Ashley will count them and that bothers him – she has been able to count well beyond five for at least two years. Still, it cannot be helped: five will have to do. Perhaps the colour will stun her so she forgets to count. And he has the watch, her real present, in his jacket pocket.

He is still angry when he thinks about it. Not about the present as such, but about the options. He should have known. Innocent as he had been when he first met Fiona, she had opened his eyes to some of the facts of life – *the* facts of life, as she sees it. He corrects himself. Innocent is not a word she would have used. Complicitous? Would that be it?

"Patriarchy," she had said the very first time she spoke to him and the Scottish vowel sound of the first syllable made the concept so warm and friendly that he had paid scant attention to what followed – something about assumptions and taking things for granted. Instead he had let her accent caress him while he focused on the light in her eyes and the glow of her cheeks and her striking auburn hair; yes, she was truly beautiful. Fortunately, he had not had so much to drink that he told her or else that would have been the end of the affair before it had even begun. There would have been no Ashley and no marriage, neither in that order nor in any other. He learned to listen in time, but it is still easy to forget exactly how pervasive *are* the facts of life.

The shop assistant had reminded him.

"These are all the rage, sir." She had pulled out a drawer. Most of the watches that came into view were heart-shaped. Pink had the upper hand over silver. He had backed away, which she must have intuited as a sign of wonder or even awe. "How old did you say your daughter was?"

"She will be six, but…"

158

"Oh, but that's perfect! We sell a lot of these to six-year-olds."

"They won't do," he had said. "I need something more neutral."

"Neutral, sir?" Her tone had indicated that she could not see how the word could be applied to watches.

"Something that isn't gender-marked," he had explained, resorting to the term Fiona had used to set his world-view, and with it his world, straight.

"You don't want a girl's watch."

"That's right. Nor a boy's watch. Something that will do for either."

"Then I'm afraid I can't help you, sir. That's all we have: girls' watches and boys' watches. And men's watches, naturally, and ladies'."

He had not given up. He had learned a long time ago, looking for clothes for Ashley, that one could often find a way around a problem.

"Might the boys' watches be less..." He had searched for the right word. "Ostentatiously gendered?"

She had pulled out another drawer. "This is what we have, sir."

On display had been an assortment of somewhat bigger watches, where hearts were conspicuously absent, as was the colour pink. Their faces showed images of vehicles mostly – cars, motorbikes.

"No bombers?" he had joked. But really, it was no joking matter. In anger he had picked up one of them. "I'll have this one."

For a moment she had seemed to hesitate. Then she had said, resolutely, no doubt taking him for a fool: "Of course. Don't forget to bring the receipt if you should wish to exchange it for something... something..."

"I won't."

"Or your wife."

"Ex," he had told her.

She had been too well trained to say what she must have been thinking: Why am I not surprised?

Now, while the bus is moving towards its destination, stopping occasionally to pick up passengers, he touches the small parcel in his pocket to make sure that it is still there, neutrally wrapped in paper that is grey and white. Neutrality is what they had always aimed for, he and Fiona, during their time together, so why buy a present that could very well serve the purpose of cross-dressing? He had been angry, if that was an excuse, and reacted spontaneously – but at that thought he stops himself. Spontaneous, as he has learned from Fiona, though her pronunciation of the stressed vowel makes that word as seductive as patriarchy, is equally problematic. "Spontaneous choices are really unchoices," she used to say, "as when people pick pink clothes for girls and blue for boys."

He looks up at the balloons as they knock gently into each other with the movements of the bus. They are all pink, the colour Fiona banned long before Ashley was born – for girls as well as boys. He has never commented on it, but Ashley's gingery fluff, still soft but darker now, closer to Fiona's auburn, would not go well with pink anyway. Green is definitely her colour. The stand with the balloons had been there as he came out of the shop; like flowers in a field, they had beckoned to him, red and blue and white and pink and yellow, pulling at their strings above the pinwheels and kites. He does not know what had possessed him. After the watch, it had seemed like a good joke. Who would seriously give Ashley six pink balloons, knowing Fiona's views? Knowing their views? Fiona will see that, won't she?

But the watch? He closes his eyes and prepares to explain – to defend, really – the choice he had made. It was

160

a courageous act of defiance, he tells himself, an attack on the stronghold of patriarchy; he has delivered a blow to its commercial centre. Never again will the poor shop assistant offer anyone a watch, unaware of its gendered nature.

Would that it were true.

He is beginning to feel as nervous as before a presentation at work.

And then another thought strikes him: what if they are not at home? What if his mother-in-law, his ex-mother-in-law to be precise, has invited them all to her house: Ashley, Fiona, Fiona's sister and husband and their two boys? It would make perfect sense: their flat, the flat he used to share with Fiona and Ashley, is on the small side. He should have called.

He does so now. Speaking to Fiona is still a strain – when he collects Ashley they exchange few words – but there is no point going all that way if they are not in.

"Colin," he says, needlessly, when she answers; unless she has deleted him, his name must have appeared on the display. "Are you at home?"

She is. And no, she is not on her way out. Her mother and father are there and so are Susan and Trevor and the boys, but of course he is welcome. Ashley has not opened her presents yet. Her granny has brought only a small gift, not the kind of huge parcel that made Ashley go all shy when she was smaller.

"Jewellery perhaps." It has been a while since Fiona was so talkative or else he would not have commented.

"She knows better than that. Perhaps it's a watch."

Colin is silent. Phone in one hand, balloons in the other, he stares in front of him. This is not fair. Still, it is just the kind of thing she would do. "Could be," he manages. What about balloons? Did she bring balloons too? Inflated with helium? He moves his thumb to "End call".

161

He is over-reacting, without a doubt, but the fact is that he has had a hard time trying to adjust to Fiona's family. Life down south had been a lot simpler in many ways. No relatives lived near enough to appear on the doorstep unannounced. For his own people, a visit would have involved a three-hour drive; for Fiona's, much more. He had had Fiona and Ashley to himself. There were friends around but none that imposed themselves on them. No one tried to come between him and Ashley. And that is what he feels his mother-in-law has been doing ever since they moved up north.

A watch of all things.

He is interrupted in his thoughts. The bus has reached the city centre and is filling up; people jostle each other, trying to grab a seat for the ride home. Some teenagers point at his balloons and giggle. "Gay," one sniggers – or that is what he hears. He would have expected that in a smaller place, but not here.

When Fiona first suggested that they should move, he had been quite unprepared. Perhaps he had been naïve. He had known that she might come to miss her family. He had known that there might be more that she missed – life on the outskirts of Maidstone must be very different from life in Edinburgh. And he could see that she might want Ashley to experience things that had been part of her own childhood. There was little he could do even for Ashley, but he tried his best. He knew only two Scottish songs, but he chose one of them for a lullaby. "Three wee craws," he sang, very quietly. "Three wee craws sat upon a wa'." She was only a wee thing herself then.

One night Fiona heard him.

"You Sassenach," she had said.

"Go paint yersel blu," he had countered, his standard rejoinder.

162

They loved each other dearly then.

After that it became Ashley's official bedtime song, a song which made her laugh, long before she understood the words, each time he brought it to a close with the fourth wee craw and a look of surprise as put-on as his accent, "He wisnae there at a'."

Colin smiles at the memory.

"I belong to Glasgow" might have been more problematic.

Now his mother-in-law is the one calling the tune, bouncing Ashley on her knee to the rhythm of *Ride a Cock Horse* – a nursery rhyme that is not even Scottish. He has been itching to tell her but has refrained – it would come across as vindictive. Nor has he said anything about the fine lady's accessories, the rings on her fingers and bells on her toes that would surely have pleased the shop assistant but turn her ladyship into a decorated doll, cock horse or not. More surprisingly, neither has Fiona.

He looks out of the window. The bus has stopped at a row of shops and a few people get off. He wonders if he should look for a different present. But what? What could he find here? There is a pub, a newsagent's, a grocer's shop, a florist – nothing that holds much promise.

Actually, moving had made good sense. Childcare was expensive. In addition, there were problems when Ashley was ill – which, in the first two years, was so often that it almost seemed to be the normal state. No sooner had she got over a cold or an ear infection than she came down with something else. Where did all the germs come from? Colin remembers nothing like it from his own childhood. Then there had been chickenpox and mumps but little else. Having no one around who could assist them did not exactly help, so Fiona had a point. Her mother, she had said, worked only part time and would be overjoyed to lend a hand.

163

She had been right. In fact, once they had both found a job – in his case a transfer – and had somewhere to live, it became evident that his mother-in-law would have loved life in the old days when there were women who were housewives and nothing else: she had become a granny almost full-time. Had there been an alternative? For not only did she look after Ashley; she also started inviting them all, her two daughters and their families, to Sunday dinner, instituting a tradition that he felt in time became something of a bind. Was this a matriarchal move or is she now imprisoned in the house of patriarchy, as Fiona would say? Except Fiona doesn't. Somehow she never seems to consider the help her mother offers in those terms.

The bus is almost empty; with a start he realizes that the next stop is his. He reaches over to press the button.

Five minutes later it is Fiona's doorbell button that he presses. She lets him in. The room where they are all assembled seems smaller than before; Fiona and he never had everybody over at the same time. He shakes hands with his parents-in-law, using their first names, which is still strange but less awkward than the other alternatives, and nods to Susan and Trevor. He hugs Ashley and ruffles the boys' hair. All the time he holds on to the balloons. He feels like a clown.

Fiona notices. She nods at the balloons.

"You can let go now, Colin. They won't take off. Why the colour?"

"I've decided I'm gay," he says, inspired by the youngsters on the bus. "Now that I've lost you."

"Gay people don't necessarily favour pink," she informs him.

"They don't?" He fakes shock. "I thought that was what defined them. Us."

"Very funny."

This is a subject his mother-in-law finds in bad taste.

"Please, Colin. Not in front of the children," she says.

Ashley is tugging at his sleeve.

"Daddy, I'm *six*," she points out.

"I know, love. Happy birthday!"

He hands over her present, but she just passes it to her mother. It is not the present she is thinking of. She is looking at the balloons.

"You're right. There should be one more. There *was* one more."

Did it break?" she asks.

He hesitates.

"No."

The slight delay has built up expectations, just as it did when he came to the final, aborted verse of her bedtime song.

"Remember the fourth wee craw?" he asks, improvising.

"The one that wisnae there?"

He nods.

"What did he do?"

"He came out of nowhere. I never even saw him. Swoosh! One moment the balloon was there, the next it was gone. It was like magic."

Ashley looks doubtful. "Then how do you know it was the crow?"

"What else could it have been? He was the only one who wasn't there."

Colin looks at her as if the logic is incontrovertible.

"So where is it now?"

"The crow?"

"The balloon, Daddy."

"Who knows?" he says. "High up, somewhere. Unless it got stuck in a tree."

And that she accepts. "I'm glad there *were* six," she says.

Fiona has set the table in the kitchen and now they all squeeze in. "Happy birthday", as always, is pitched too high – or too low – for him, but he joins in anyway. "Remember to make a wish," says Fiona, and then there is a crossfire of camera flashes as Ashley leans over the table to blow out the candles. She closes her eyes and for an instant Colin is transferred to the hospital six years ago when the nurse held her up as if for inspection, disclosing that this child, no bigger than a doll, its red skin wrinkled, its eyes screwed tightly shut, was a girl and not the boy he must have been hoping for without even being aware of it, for he had experienced, for the briefest possible moment, a twinge of disappointment. Then it had passed.

He has never told Fiona, nor, it goes without saying, Ashley. Fiona would just have found him pitiful and quoted de Beauvoir. "One is not born a woman," she would have said – which would have been beside the point. Wouldn't it?

Pieces of cake are being passed around, along with lemonade and tea. As so often in the past, Colin notes how different the children are. The boys, seven and five, are messy eaters, particularly Sean, the older of the two. He has spilled lemonade and bits of icing from his cake all over the place. Ashley is neat and methodical. Colin wonders again if this is because she is a girl. Fiona would deny it. "It's because girls are brought up to be neat," she would say. "With boys, people don't bother." Is that what they should have done, he and Fiona – not bothered? To offset the influence of everybody else they would have had to do more than that; they would have had to actually encourage sloppiness. "Attagirl!" they would have had to say, using the American phrase rather than a meek "There's a good

166

girl". "Never mind the mess. It's good to see that you're enjoying your food."

"Time to open your presents, Ashley."

It is Fiona's voice. She must have been waiting for everyone to finish but has now given up on the boys. They have left enough on their plates for an additional child.

"Let me clear the table first." Her mother gets up.

"I'll do it," Colin offers.

"You are both guests," says Fiona. "Pass me your plates, please, all of you." She stacks the dirty dishes by the sink and wipes the table. "There." She turns to Ashley. "Do you want to start with Daddy's?"

This must be for having referred to him as a guest.

But Ashley wants to keep his till last. Colin is pleased even though the gesture could mean anything.

She picks up her grandparents' gift. It is bigger than his, but could still be a watch. What else would grandparents give a six-year-old if they want something that will last a little longer than toys or clothes? He hopes Fiona is wrong. Perhaps it is a mobile phone or a camera. She is too young for either, but you never know these days.

Ashley removes the string and then winds it into a ball. She puts it on the table where it immediately unwinds. She is about to pick it up again when Fiona takes it. She must be as curious as he is.

Was Ashley always so meticulous? He thinks not. Now she loosens the paper carefully, straightening the creases as she unfolds it. Inside is a box. She opens it.

"A doll!" Her face lights up.

"A doll?" Fiona looks at her mother. "I thought…"

"It's not just a doll, Fiona." Her mother is defensive. She sounds like someone demonstrating kitchen gadgets in a department store: It's not just a potato peeler. If you… "It's a collectible," she says.

167

"What's that, Granny?" asks Ashley.

"It's still a doll," Fiona insists.

"Well, in a manner of speaking. But it's not a toy."

"Can't I play with it?" asks Ashley. "What's it for then?"

"I give up," says Fiona. "I don't know how often…"

Colin is not certain he wants to intervene, but does. "It's not the end of the world, is it? It's only a doll. Pretty, if you like dolls."

"First pink balloons and now a doll. What next? A make-up kit?" Fiona tends to resort to sarcasm when she is angry. "Would you give one to Sean, Mum?" She looks accusingly at her mother.

"Listen, young lady." Her father's tone is sharp. "Don't be so ungrateful. Your mother went to a lot of trouble to find something she thought Ashley would like not only now but when she gets older. There are whole sets of these Victorian miniature dolls and they're quite valuable."

"I'm sorry, Dad, but you know my views. Our views," she adds, including Colin.

"Let's not argue today," he says. "It's Ashley's birthday."

But that is clearly irrelevant.

"Whose side are you on?" she asks.

"Do there have to be sides?" Susan's question, at any other time, would have led to something resembling a lecture, but now Fiona gives in, it seems.

"Have it your way."

She sounds resigned, but Colin knows that this is not the end of it as far as she is concerned. Ashley, though, takes it that the present is no longer an issue. She moves around the table to give her granny and grandpa a hug. Her granny pulls her close, holding her just a little longer than necessary. "My baby," she says. It is as if they are in collusion.

And then Ashley picks up Susan's gift, which turns out to be wholly sensible: a pad to draw on – colouring books tend to be gendered, Colin knows, depicting either princesses or knights in armour – and a set of felt pens in all shades and hues. Ashley hugs both Susan and Trevor.

"What did you get from Mummy?" Colin asks. He feels tense after Fiona's reaction to her parents' present and wants to divert attention from his, which Ashley has placed in front of her. She has started rolling up the string with the same precise movements as before.

"An anorak," she says. "It's for the autumn. It has a zip instead of buttons and it's green. I got to try it on in the shop. I like it."

"Good. Maybe I can see it later."

"Yes."

The string unrolls again but this time both Fiona and Ashley leave it where it is. Colin pockets it. Give me enough rope, he thinks. There is nothing like a bit of drama to liven up a birthday.

"I hope you'll like mine too." His mouth is dry.

"Yes," says Ashley.

She has removed the paper and opens the box.

"Yes," she says again, this time with emphasis. "Yes, I do."

And she lifts his present out of the box and holds it in her hand. The white skull and crossbones stand out in sharp contrast to the shiny black watch face. The leather strap is a solid black against her pink palm. Her eyes sparkle.

On the bus, with no balloons to hold, he takes the piece of string out of his pocket and twists it around his finger. He no longer knows why he had been so worried. What could have gone wrong, really?

His mother-in-law had been about to say something, he

169

knows, but had got no further than "But—" Had her husband nudged her? Regardless, no one would have heard her – the loud "wow" from the boys would have drowned her out.

"Oh Mum, can I have one? It'll soon be my birthday." Sean had been pulling at his mother's arm.

Ron had been hopping up and down. "Me too, me too!"

Fiona had given Colin a look he could not read. Was it an expression of dejection? He did not know. He had shrugged his shoulders.

"I liked the design," he lied.

"A skull and crossbones?"

"It's striking. If you want to, you can look at it symbolically. It's a sort of *memento mori*. Quite fitting for a timepiece, don't you think?"

"For a six-year-old?"

"Why not?"

"What's a *memento mori*?" Ashley had asked. She had stumbled on the unfamiliar phrase.

"A sort of reminder, love," he had answered. "A reminder that time is passing."

Fiona had looked at him. "I take it that's a cue."

"Yes. I should be on my way."

"Jojo has one like it," Ashley had said. It was clear that it meant a lot to her.

"Jojo?" Fiona had sounded curious.

"Yes. And Philip too."

"Who is Jojo?"

"You know, Josephine. She's in my class. Her dad calls her Jojo."

"And Jojo has one?"

"Yes. And Fern has a notebook with skulls and crossbones on the cover. Her mum gave it to her. She's to write in it when she's angry."

170

"I see," Fiona had said. "That's nice."

Colin had been able to tell that she was confused. She was rarely even close to monosyllabic unless she was deep in thought.

"Who else?" she had asked.

"No one else. No one else has a watch. Now they'll all want one!"

Colin had tried to fasten it around her wrist, but the strap needed another hole. Fiona had no awl – the toolkit had been his – but had passed him a darning needle as well as a knitting needle from her sewing box, so that he could first pierce the strap and then enlarge the hole. When he was done, Ashley had danced into the living room with her hands high in the air.

And Fiona had turned to him. "Well, it made her happy. I'd never have looked twice at a watch like that. It seems so obviously meant for boys. How did you know?"

Without the least hesitation he lied for the second time. "I never gave it a thought," he said. "Why shouldn't girls be pirates? I just took it for granted she'd like it. Any child would."

The piece of string Colin has been toying with is getting entangled. He puts it back in his pocket. Soon he will be home – the driver is making good time. Someday, he thinks, he should give not Ashley but Fiona six pink balloons. No. A dozen. That would stun her. He calls her.

"Colin," he says again. "I just wanted to thank you."

"That's all right. I suppose it went as well as could be expected, considering."

"Yes." He does not ask her to explain what she means. Instead he says: "We didn't really have much of a chance to talk."

"Colin, it was Ashley's birthday party."

171

"Yes, of course. Some other time, perhaps?"

"Of course."

"I could bring balloons."

"Whatever for?"

"It was meant as a joke," he says.

"Right."

"Next week?"

"I think we should leave it a bit longer, Colin."

"Yes, perhaps. I'll be in touch."

"Right."

"Cheers."

"Cheers."

Thirteen, he decides; thirteen balloons, not twelve. A baker's dozen. The last one for luck, in case he needs it. With women, you never know. You just never know.

Moe

The tiger holds her, its eyes cold, distant. Mesmerized, she blocks the man's way, paying no heed to the rush-hour crowd around them. "Truly amazing." Her words come in a whisper. "So lifelike. So in control." Due to the man's tan, even the colour is right. "Where did you have it done?" With his shirt unbuttoned halfway down his chest, exposing most of the tiger's head, the question doesn't feel intrusive.

"You like it?"

She confirms that she does.

"It was either that or a wolf."

"I'm a cat lover myself. Dogs I can do without."

"So you'd have picked the tiger, too."

She hesitates.

"A cub, perhaps."

His is full-grown; it needs a chest twice the size of hers. Three times. She casts a quick glance at the man's face. He's neither wolf, nor tiger. His hair, unkempt, might turn into a lion's mane if left to grow, but is a little dark. He has a drawn look.

But if he's tired, he isn't the least bashful. There's a pub around the corner, he says. How about they drop in? To her surprise, she accepts. And though they split after one drink, they exchange not only names but phone numbers. Elaine. Gene.

So it goes.

Engrossed in thoughts of the tiger, she arrives home, checks her mail. None. Miriam welcomes her, while Alice and Misha hang back. "Salmon today," she tells them, having stopped at the Co-op on the way home. She takes her shopping into the kitchenette, cleans the cats' tray to get rid of the smell, feeds them.

Eeny, Meeny, Miny, Moe had been their names when

173

there were four of them, but having lost Moe, she renamed the others so as not to be reminded constantly that her favourite was gone. Now, in spite of that, the children's counting rhyme comes to mind – catch a tiger. Catch a tiger by the toe. But will Gene's tiger really have toes?

If it does, they'll be down by his knees. She sees them move with each step he takes, as he walks along a sunlit beach, and giggles.

In the days that follow, she recharges her phone more often than is strictly necessary, but to no avail: he doesn't call. Yet he was the one who'd asked for her number. Of course, he may do that with everyone he meets. He may add names to his contact list just to impress his mates. Come to think of it, he may have got the number wrong. If she doesn't hear from him by Saturday, she could give him a ring. She could, couldn't she?

No. She should wait a full week.

After all, what had they talked about? The tiger, that was it.

The tiger and some friend of his who'd died.

Her own loss had been on the tip of her tongue, but she had kept it to herself. You don't vie for sympathy. But it's hard to know what to say at an unplanned first meeting.

Not anything personal, for sure.

I'm thirty-nine. I have three cats. I'm a receptionist. That would have been quite safe. But would it have defined her?

No more than if she'd stated her real age.

And what would define him? His tiger?

She'll give him a week and after that delete his number.

She goes to work, comes home and feeds the cats. Eventually, the absence of a call is lost among all other absences.

"Chicken today," she tells Miriam, who winds herself around her legs, purring contentedly.

174

And then, once she has stopped recharging her phone daily, she hears from him – or, to be more precise, he texts her. "Djcu although k civic ncjckvfjdcjv high djfif," she reads. No "hi, hello, how are you", no signature. Had she deleted him as she'd been of a mind to do, she wouldn't have had a clue who it came from; since she didn't, the display shows his name. She stares at the three proper words; she tries to figure out what the rest could mean. Is this some kind of code? If so, what could "ncjckvfjdcjv" stand for – twelve consonants in a row? Why isn't all of it in code?

Frustrated, she puts the phone down, deciding to ignore it. It could be his idea of a joke.

Unless the text has been jumbled in transit.

She'd better reply. "Hi," she writes. "It seems your tiger got hold of the phone. May I suggest you trim his claws." Having added her name, she presses down on "send".

His reply is almost instantaneous. "Just warming up. Letting my fingers dance, to see what might come of it." She has no more than glanced at his message when he is on the phone. Now there's a "hi, how are you" followed by a few bland phrases. Even so, after saying next to nothing, they arrange to meet.

So much for her reserve.

The third time they come together, she learns, to her disappointment, that there are no toes to the tiger; there's no body at all. Lying on her side, she traces the outline of the neck that isn't there, the missing chest and legs, moving down one side and up the other, rounding each of his knees in turn, gliding over the crotch. She also learns that Gene is estranged from his wife.

"Wife," she says. Her hand stops in mid-air. The wife stands over them.

175

"Estranged," he repeats, as if that was the salient fact. "We don't see eye to eye."

She draws her hand back. "And so you've left her." It's not a question, but the ensuing silence lasts much longer than it should, turning it into one.

She is the one who finally breaks it. "You're saying that you haven't left her."

"I did, for a while. I moved in with a friend. But he died. I told you."

Not as it related to his wife, he hadn't, but no matter. Does he expect her to commiserate?

"I'm a sort of lodger. It simplifies matters."

"Sort of."

"Yes." He turns towards her. "Look, it's a temporary arrangement. It gives me a bed. It provides me with an address. That's all."

Sort of, she thinks; but she doesn't repeat the phrase. Would he have told her if there'd been more to it? An address. A mattress. Given the housing situation, countless people must remain together who would much rather live apart, having fallen out of love.

"Anyway, I never loved her," he points out, as if to correct her thoughts.

And she leaves it at that.

"Make me feel you," he says.

She does.

He's an artist, he informs her.

She had been complaining about the mess at work. The stress. His non sequitur tells her it doesn't interest him. "You paint?" she asks.

"I did some graffiti as a kid. The council had it removed. But being an artist isn't about what you do. It's a state of mind."

He's sitting on the bed, his feet on the floor, petting

176

Misha. Alice is watching him. So is Miriam, who is keeping an eye on both.

"How?"

"A way of seeing things."

"You mean aesthetically?"

His hand waves away the suggestion and Misha is gone. "Aesthetics have nothing to do with it. It's an awareness of disruptions, of connections. An openness to patterns, patterns that form and disintegrate. To chaos. You know."

Does she? She isn't sure.

"It's not what you do?"

"That will reflect it. But what means you use is immaterial. Paint, you said. Sure. Performance. Film. Photography. Music. Writing."

"Clay," she offers.

"If you want."

Miriam has approached him; she arches her back, rubbing against his leg. Gene puts down his hand and she butts it with her head. Then, without warning, as his thumb strokes her, she bites him. He pulls away with an oath.

Elaine scoops up the cat. "I'm sorry. She's not herself." Holding the cat out of his reach, she inspects the cut. There are a few spots of blood. "You'd better clean it under the tap. I'll get you a plaster." She puts the cat down.

"No need. I'll stay clear of her in future."

"She's probably jealous."

"Well, I won't pet the others either."

Because of me, she'd meant. But she keeps it to herself.

There are no plasters in the bathroom, but she finds one in her handbag. Photography, music, writing, he'd said. "Are you doing anything now?" she asks, returning. "Writing, for example?"

"On and off. I've put down one or two six-word stories lately."

She must have shown her ignorance.

"*He kissed her,*" he says. "*That changed nothing.*"

She remains nonplussed.

"*He kissed him,*" he says. "*That changed everything.*"

She sticks the plaster on his arm, pats it down.

"It started with Hemingway. An American writer."

"William," she declares.

"That was Faulkner. He wrote a story in the form of a sales ad, about a pair of baby shoes that had never been worn. Six words. You're left to figure out why."

"That's sad."

"I used the idea for one of mine. *Closing-down sale. World ends at noon.*"

"The baby shoes are more moving." He flinches; it's not what he wanted to hear. "Of course, it's a bit limited," she adds, making amends. "Are you planning to do a whole book?"

She works out what it would take. With thirty lines to the page, even a slim volume could hold thousands of stories. Who would want to write that many? Who would want to read them?

"You'd probably need illustrations to break it up a bit."

"Stories of one hundred words each would be an alternative. It would be easier. The shorter they are, the greater the challenge."

"I have one," she says. Her fingers mark the rhythm as she counts. "She kept his tiger up all night. Four."

He corrects her. "Seven. And overly optimistic. I have to be on my way." All the same he pulls her down beside him.

They meet at irregular intervals and always, as soon as their initial dates are disposed of, at her place. Mostly this is every few days, but sometimes a week or two will pass between visits. He doesn't stay the night. She wonders why. Once bitten, twice shy, she reckons – and it's his marriage she is thinking of, not Miriam. But they wouldn't have to get married. And if it isn't that, if it's the size of her flat that worries him, as she suspects, it shouldn't be impossible to find a slightly larger place if they really set their hearts on it. One more room would do. It would be one step up from the bed he occupies at his ex-wife's place. Well, ex-wife-to-be, maybe – Elaine still isn't sure they are divorced.

Early on, after he had been away for a while, she let him know she missed him. "Don't count the days," he texted back. "Make the days count."

"Witty," she replied, "but how can I, all on my own?"

He has a store of clichéd phrases, the kind you find set in cheap frames in bric-a-brac shops. "Today's the first day of the rest of your life" is one of them. Hearing it, she'd made a face in response, which had offended him. "What's wrong with it?" he'd said. "It's true, isn't it?"

Yet all his visits occur at the end of the day and present nothing like a new beginning. He doesn't take her out. He's frowned at cinemas, pubs, theatres. Here is where they belong, accompanied by her three cats.

At least, she concludes, he is considerate. He doesn't turn up unannounced. He doesn't let her down. If something intervenes, he texts her, though without stating the reason. It's not that he is secretive exactly, but as if she occupies, as if he would like to see her occupy, a sphere of her own, drifting above whatever else there is. She should be grateful, shouldn't she?

Therefore, she is surprised when, after a few months, he offers something of an excuse. Her phone bleeps and the message reads: "Sorry. Can't get away. Will be in touch."

Can't get away. It must be from home – there's nowhere else for him to get away from, as far as she knows. So what could keep him there? Nothing that she can think of. It won't be his wife, unless their relations are very different

179

from what he has implied. What if there is a child? His wife's? That must be it. No wonder they're estranged; she must have had an affair and got pregnant. But would he babysit someone else's child? It sounds unlikely. Perhaps it's not his wife's. Perhaps some friend of his had no one to turn to at short notice and left his child with him. Just for an hour or two. Would he? Please? She can't imagine him doing it professionally. Well, maybe. The one time she'd approached him about work, he had implied he takes what comes his way, on a short-term basis, to remain as free as possible. He's an artist. Babysitting could be an option. Being watched over by a tiger would make any child happy.

No. That isn't the Gene she knows.

"Ditch him," says Olivia, who isn't a close friend but someone she can trust to a degree. "He comes to be fed and have sex, right? In that or any other order."

The summary leaves out so much. Being two.

"Right?"

Elaine nods, reluctantly.

"Do you sew on his buttons for him, too?"

"There's been no need. He wears his shirts unbuttoned, pretty much."

Olivia winces. "Ditch him."

If he hollers.

But he hasn't hollered, has he? He's just not been around a whole lot lately.

He wouldn't babysit. There is no child. Can't be.

Two weeks go by. Three. It's autumn now and after work Elaine busies herself washing and putting away her summer clothes, cleaning the windows, giving the kitchenette a thorough scrub. She considers buying heavy curtains for the winter, to keep out the draught. The warmth would be welcome. At the same time, their newness might entice the cats to start their climbing tricks again. She's in two minds.

It's rare she gives Gene a conscious thought.

Four weeks.

That's when he contacts her, acknowledging that it has been a while. "Hi," reads his message. "Long time no see. How about tonight?"

No can do, she should reply. But she deflects Olivia's advice and welcomes him. This time, the first time ever, he brings sardines for Miriam.

They make love. The tiger, she notes, has paled – Gene's tan is all but gone.

She feeds him.

Casually, between mouthfuls – or such is her intention – she asks how he's been doing, avoiding the word "what". "Kept busy?" She pours more water into her glass, focussing on the task. Miriam, she notes, is watching him.

"On and off," he tells her. "You know how it is."

She doesn't, but he has shut the door on her. The only insight she has gained into his work concerns his story fragments. She tries to ease it open.

"And the child?"

The result is a blank look. Soundlessly Miriam sways her tail from side to side.

"The child," he repeats, but without a question mark.

"I took it you were babysitting."

"You did?" Again there's an extended pause before he continues. "Actually, there are two. Two girls."

"Your wife's."

"Yes." This time the pause that follows is quite short. "And mine."

"But I wasn't to know?"

"I'd rather not go into it." He pushes his chair back, gets up. "As I said, I'm little more than a lodger."

181

Little more than. "A sort of" was the phrase he'd used before. How little more? Olivia was right.

"It's kind of you to help out with your children. Keeping your marriage afloat."

But why use sarcasm? It won't change anything. She watches him as he moves towards the hall. He gets into his shoes, his jacket. With his back to her he zips it up. He turns around. Hidden from sight, it is as if the tiger no longer exists.

"All good things come to an end," he says. He leaves the door to the flat gaping and heads for the stairs. Remaining in her seat, she listens to the echo of his steps, accompanied by the humming of a tune. He's never done that before. Could he be working on a song? As he reaches the ground floor, there is a squeaky sound followed almost immediately by a bang. Then all sounds cease.

Her tail held high, Miriam goes over to her bowl. She'll have her sardines now.

Some ten days before Christmas Elaine catches sight of him not far from where they first met. Walking beside him is a girl, too young to be his wife, too old to be his daughter. He has his arm around her and they kiss. Decidedly no daughter. She shrugs. That changes nothing. She is done with him.

And so, a week later, when her phone bleeps as she is getting ready to go home for her brief holiday, the staff party over, Gene couldn't be further from her mind. Seeing that the message is from him, she contemplates deleting it unread. Quite possibly he'd seen her in the street, observing him; kissing the girl may have been merely for show, to provoke her. Will he be texting her that there are more fish in the sea? Should she read it?

Curiosity gets the better of her. But if he had in fact seen her, he doesn't let on. What meets her eyes is longer than anything he's sent her before and has the appearance of a

182

poem rather than a message produced in a rush. There's even a title of sorts: "For You." Having glanced through it, she starts again from the top:

"So what went wrong?"
"Well, nothing, really. It just didn't work out."
"He didn't…?"
"No."
"What a shame. Still, you'd kept your flat, hadn't you?"
"Yes. And the cats."
"The cats?"
"Yes."
"You didn't consider…?"
"No."
"Perhaps you should have."
"I just couldn't. And then it was too late."
"How many…?"
"Why?"
"You're right."
"Anyway, I'm glad now."
"You are?"
"They're company."
"I can imagine."
"So is the dog."
"You have a dog as well?"
"It was his. He told me he liked dogs."
"And left it with you?"
"Yes."
"Good riddance, I would say."
"Yeah, I suppose."

She's puzzled. Is this meant to be her? She and who else? A casual acquaintance? Someone who doesn't know she has three cats? And what is she to make of it? Recalling his comments on very short texts, she counts the words and notes that with the title they add up to one hundred. One of his hundred-word stories. She is flattered, till she remembers that six words were a greater challenge. That takes away some of the glow. "World ends at noon." Still. The story is dedicated to her. In a manner of speaking. "To Elaine" would have been more of a tribute than "For You".

Arriving home, again with cat food in her bag, she finds a small brown and white dog, some kind of terrier, possibly part Jack Russell, tied to the banister outside her door. A tag bears the inscription "For Elaine". She sighs. Gene. But why? As if she, who already has three cats, could raise a dog – a dog which has to be taken out three, four times a day. She is a working woman. Having untied it, she picks it up and unlocks the door. She is met by Miriam, who arches her back. "We'll have none of that," she says, shooing her out of the way. "He's a guest." He? She?

Eeny, Meeny, Miny, Moe – that's who they used to be.

The janitor at work could maybe keep it in his room during the day, so she can walk it in her lunch hour. She'll have to give it some thought.

Whatever she decides, she'd better go slow.

Moe.

Erasing the past.

"Meeny," she calls. And Miriam steals up to her. "Meet Moe." And she puts the dog down carefully, shielding it with her arm. There. Just in case.

The Real Thing

I watched him from the door but wasn't sure. His general build was about right. The changes were those you would expect in a seventy-year-old: a slight stoop, a waistline that had gone from concave to convex, the chin a little saggy. In that he resembled his replacement – his most recent replacement, if you side with those who argue that there have been several. His hairstyle was different from his twenty-five-year-old self, but his nose looked much the same, the tip perhaps a bit droopy. I couldn't see his eyes, but I suspected they would have lost the shine they'd had the second year at Newport. It happens to us all.

Not much to go by, you say, and you are right. In fact, I'll level with you. I wasn't exactly on a pub crawl, but I'd had a few. I may not have been the best judge. And the scene wasn't one where you'd expect to find someone like him. In spite of its name, The Star was hardly a place for stars, nor former stars, who I suspect might be even more particular about their surroundings. And why England? Mexico would have been more likely. At the same time, the whole thing seemed fated in a way. I'd never set foot in the pub before, but someone happened to throw the door open as I left its neighbour, The Dark Horse, so I walked in. One last stop, I'd decided, on the spur of the moment. Once inside, I noticed him right away, up by the counter, and then not even wild horses and so on and so forth. He was on his own, his shoulders raised – shielding his identity, was the impression I got – both hands around the glass. He was nursing his beer.

That threw me. Was beer his drink? What came to mind was burgundy, followed, perhaps, as in the song, by the harder stuff, but then people change. With Keith Richards you could most likely bank on Jack Daniels, but not everyone is so set in their ways.

"Another one," I said to the barman as I reached the counter. I steadied the stool before it fell. "Bitter," I added.

"*Jawohl.*" I could have sworn he clicked his heels together. "Coming up."

Why did he take me for German?

Then I turned my head to get a better view. I could be wrong. A man and a woman hid much of him, but as I said, his general build, his waistline, his chin and nose were about right.

Of course, most of those who see today's version as a copy would not have given him a second look, being convinced that he died in that motorcycle accident in 1966, but I never thought so. McCartney, yes. It's common knowledge that there was friction between him and the others in the band. When he walked out of the studio and got into his car, it must have been obvious to them all that he was about to quit – which would have put an end to everything. An educated guess says that if he did, he had to be gone for good. The look-alike that was available must have made things easier. But Dylan? No way. There would have been no need for drastic action. If he'd decided that he'd had enough, he would hardly have objected to someone else stepping into his shoes. He would probably have seen it as a good joke. Being Dylan must have become quite a burden. If you don't believe me you should check the film of his 1965 tour. "God, I'd hate to be me," he says, or something like it, reading what the papers have written about him. Discarding the Dylan identity must have been a relief. He would be free to do anything. Who knows how many lives he's lived since then?

In a way I pity those who bought the official story. How much less exciting must it not be to believe that he had simply taken time out and then returned with new energy. Mind you, it suits their narrow-mindedness and that is presumably why they react with such hostility if I pass a slighting remark on the Dylan of today. "It's not him," I might say. "Can't you see? It's not him?" But how convince them? They simply dismiss my arguments as "nothing but conspiracy theories". Nothing but! As if there would be conspiracy theories if there were no conspiracies! One goes with the other, right? Then they bring up the moon landings. "You think they were a conspiracy too?" they say, as if Dylan and McCartney and the moon landings were all of a kind. They should check the evidence on the Internet.

In 1966 that wasn't an option. I wish it had been. In fact, I wish the Internet had existed in 1962. If it had been available when Dylan first started out, it would have been a godsend to anyone who took his music seriously – in those days there were no printed lyrics, neither on the back of an album nor as an insert, and Dylan's were no exception. There was just nowhere one could find the words. I still remember lying on the floor close to the speaker of my portable record player, pencil in hand, trying to catch them. I had to get them down. They spoke to me. I'm not exaggerating when I say that Dylan hit me harder than puberty.

It's not surprising then that when he disappeared after the accident, it hurt. I may have been especially vulnerable because of my age – I was sixteen – but living in uncertainty also made matters worse. If his death had been confirmed, I could have gone through the different stages of grief, from denial to acceptance, as others did with Hendrix and Joplin and the rest. As it was, all I could mourn was his absence. The many substitutes that appeared over the years were never able to make up for the loss. I'm not saying that they didn't have their good points, a number of them. But they weren't the real thing.

In a way I never got over it. Many is the time I dreamt

about him and woke to a feeling of disappointment after chasing a shadowy image through circuses and crowded kitchens, skirting pots of boiling fat. I never once had a clear view of him.

Until the night I'm talking about.

The couple were finally done. I finished my beer and moved sideways, glass in hand, to catch the barman's attention. "Same again, please." Then I turned to the person I was almost sure was Dylan.

"Quiet tonight." I gave him a quick glance.

"I wouldn't know."

Ah, subtle.

"You haven't been here before?"

He shook his head. "Uh-uh."

"You from the States?" I asked.

"Listen, I just want to enjoy my beer," he said. This time he faced me.

"Sure."

His accent troubled me. It was American, but was this how Dylan would sound after nearly fifty years? He'd grown up in the Midwest, but even at the start of his career he'd moved around a lot. I found it hard to imagine him settled in one place after that. To tell the truth, even if he had, if I'd had positive proof that he'd lived in New York since 1966, it wouldn't have helped: I couldn't – I can't – tell a New Yorker from a Midwesterner. They are both pretty nasal, aren't they? Now, if I'd been talking to someone else, some woman, say, or someone who mattered less, I might not have been so tongue-tied. I could have improvised. I might have said I had a cousin in Minnesota who sounded like her. Well, almost. "Really," she would say. "I'm from Washington." "State?" I would ask. "D.C.?" But with him I had to be careful. He would be sure to leave at the first sign that I recognized him.

At the same time, I had to do something. He might leave anyway. He might simply finish his beer, give me a nod and then head for the door. He might not even nod. I had to find out if I was right. I waited, searching for an opening that wouldn't make him suspicious. Given his reserve so far, I obviously had my work cut out for me.

"Sorry I bothered you," is what I came up with. "I talk too much, right? I'm Robert. My friends call me Bob."

They don't, since I'm not his namesake, but I was hoping it might catch him off guard.

"Hi," he said, making a face. "Rob."

But getting the cold shoulder didn't faze me.

"That yours?" I asked, not letting on that I got the point. To my surprise he actually answered.

"You can call me Al."

Ah! He very definitely had Dylan's sense of humour – who else would have thought of quoting a fellow artist? But then it struck me: before Dylan became Dylan, his middle name had been Allen. Robert Allen Zimmerman. With Bob and presumably Robert gone, Allen would be what remained. Allen. Al. Two initials: A. Z. That about covered the alphabet. A to Z. The A to Z guide to what? Except he would hardly be Zimmerman any more.

"That's a good one," I said.

Even from the side I could tell he was offended.

"I meant the song," I explained. "Paul Simon's song. *You Can Call Me Al.*"

He shrugged. "I don't listen to a lot of music."

What was he telling me? That he wasn't much of a listener? That there was music he wouldn't listen to?

"You never did?" I asked, playing it safe. "What about Rock-a-day Johnny? Fabian? Martha and the Vandellas?"

The names may have come out a bit slurred – quite a mouthful, that. I tried them a second time. But if he recognized my allusion to the different versions of *Talkin'* *World War III Blues* he didn't let on.

"I've heard some."

I waited, but that was all he said.

"When you were younger, you mean?"

He may have nodded.

I changed tack.

"So what are you doing here?"

He looked at me. "The obvious. Relaxing over a beer. Or trying to."

"Sorry. I meant in England."

"In England." He paused for so long that I wondered if that was it. Then he said: "You could say I'm waiting for my ship to come in."

Yes! This was a clear hint! Anybody who'd ever listened to Dylan would catch the reference to his song.

"But the hour isn't here?" I proposed. It was the best I could come up with. Given my state, I was less quick-witted than I would be under normal circumstances.

"Wouldn't seem like it."

I'd obviously missed the chance to connect. His reply gave me no opening. Soon he would be on his way and there was nothing I could do about it. "Can I get you another beer?" I asked, making the obvious move. In a flash of inspiration I added: "Or maybe you'd prefer some of the harder stuff."

"I don't do drugs," he said.

I was taken aback. Was that what the song suggested? Not spirits? I shook my head. "I meant something like whisky. Brandy. Tequila."

"I'm fine with beer," he answered. "Thanks."

Was that a yes? Rather than ask, I signalled to the barman, pointing to our glasses. There was no need to invite a rebuff. I remembered how truculent he used to be in interviews.

190

We didn't say anything for a while. Well, I didn't, with the result that the conversation, what little there had been of it, died – Dylan, if it was him, hadn't exactly warmed to my attempts to get him to open up. Suddenly I didn't mind. It felt good sitting there beside him. What more did I need? The place had filled up since I arrived, but the crowd wasn't all that noisy. The light was pleasantly dim. The beer tasted good.

But I must have wanted more. When I spoke again it was to say: "You remind me of someone." It wasn't something I had planned – it just came out. You must have done that too: that's what happens when you relax over a beer or two. Your thoughts run away with you. Before you realize it, you're even ahead of your thoughts. I've seen people end up married that way.

"I do?" he said. "And who would that be?"

"I'm not sure. Help me out."

"How can I? Besides, I might prefer not to be told."

Only if you don't want to be recognized, was on the tip of my tongue. This was almost a confession, wasn't it?

"How come?"

"People make all sorts of comparisons. You can't let that bother you."

"You'll remain as you are regardless?"

"That's right."

"Dylan," I said.

"Eh?"

I'd expected some sort of reaction, but there was none. If anything, he was puzzled.

"Dylan said that. In one of his early songs."

"He can't have been the only one."

For me he was, I wanted to say. But I didn't – he wouldn't want me crying in my beer. Instead I nodded agreement. "But it must have mattered a lot more to him than it does to most people. Why else write a song about it? I'll be who I am and not give a damn. Bye-bye. 'Restless Farewell.' You know?"

My sideways glance was meant to show that I understood his situation and that he had nothing to fear, but all I got was: "I won't argue with you. You're the expert, it seems." And then he sipped at his beer, totally unconcerned.

Forty-six years since he vanished. No, forty-seven. I could have been more precise, but it might have taken me a few minutes: the date didn't make for easy maths. July 29, 1966. "Restless Farewell" had been released two years before that. Had he forgotten what it was about? Had he put it out of his mind? He must have.

I excused myself to go to the gents. When I came back, he appeared to be deep in thought, so I decided not to intrude. Instead I studied the bottles behind the bar. I started to count them, but their reflections in the mirror that formed their background made it difficult. The barman gave me a questioning look. I realized that I'd been pointing at them as I counted and shook my head. "No, thanks." My speech had probably thickened a bit; I may have been approaching the stage where the syllables do somersaults.

I waited. I think I can say that I'm more patient than most, but, of course, I still wanted to find out. The waiting had to come to an end. I had to get him to talk. "Perhaps I've met you somewhere," I ventured. I tried to hide the urgency I felt.

"You what?"

I repeated the phrase. The bar had grown noisier. It was getting late, so there were more young people around.

"Perhaps," he replied.

"Where could that have been?"

"You're asking me where I spend my time?"

"Yes."

Was he troubled or merely irritated?

"I know." I nodded. "It's none of my business."

"You're right," he said. But then he must have changed his mind: he mentioned a few places I'd never heard of along with some I had. "I go here, there and everywhere."

"Mexico," I repeated.

"Yes, that's one of them. You been there?"

"No. I don't do much travelling."

He looked at me strangely. "So we haven't met."

I had to agree. "Apparently not," I said.

From that point on my memory is hazy. Time speeded up, as it tends to do when you're drinking, but I can still recollect more or less how we ended up at my place. Basically, it was the barman's doing. I wanted another whisky but couldn't seem to catch his eye. When he finally took my order, I nodded in Dylan's direction, just to be friendly. "You know who he reminds me of?"

"I have no idea," said the barman. "Dustin Hoffman?"

I leaned my head sideways. I couldn't see it. "No." I shook my head. "No way. He's Bob Dylan."

The barman shrugged his shoulders. "If you say so."

"Not the one who's around today," I explained. "I mean the real Dylan. The one who disappeared after the accident." But the barman had disappeared too.

Dylan furrowed his brow. "Are you sure you should drink that?" he asked.

"I'm fine," I said.

But apparently I wasn't. When I wanted one last drink, or maybe it was the one after that, to round things off, the barman turned to Dylan, reading into my earlier comment a greater familiarity than there were grounds for, perhaps.

"You should see your friend home," he told him.

I'm not sure what else was said – there may have been

some kind of argument and I may have been involved in it – but after a while I found myself outside in the fresh air.

"You *are* the real Dylan, aren't you?" I asked.

And now he didn't bother to deny it.

The rest of the evening, as I said, is hazy. Some things I can still recall, but others have left no trace. We set off towards my place on foot, but at some point Dylan must have hailed a taxi. I remember having problems getting into it. I remember having problems getting out. I wanted to pay, but he wouldn't let me.

We sang – or was it only I who sang? Was this on the way home or was it later? I can still see in my mind's eye the taxi driver drumming on the steering wheel of his car, but was this done to music or simply to mark time? When I woke in the late morning, still fully dressed, sprawled across the living room sofa, the first verse of *Black Crow Blues* was going round and round in my head, endlessly, the piano as hard as a hammer, as if on constant repeat. Weary is not the word for it. I saw my guitar propped up against a chair, a book of sheet music on the table, open, not as I would have expected, to that song but – and it took an effort to make out the words – to *Just Like Tom Thumb's Blues*. Had I asked him what the title meant? An ashtray spoke of a very late night. Who had smoked? I stopped years ago, but if I'd had a relapse, it would account for the headache and the state of my mouth and throat, at least in part. The cigarettes must have been Dylan's. He used to smoke, of course, but did he still? At the pub, had he gone out to have a cigarette when I went to the gents? There were also glasses and an empty bottle of malt on the table. Still, apart from the ashtray, the scene was no worse than any other morning after an evening out. Had I made my neighbour bang on the wall again?

Dylan was nowhere around.

I went back to bed – or rather, I went to bed. Sleep didn't come easy, needless to say. *Black Crow Blues* had run its course but left no vacuum; instead, the questions that I should have asked, that I must have asked, fought for space. What exactly happened on that day in July forty-seven years ago? When he made his decision to opt out, did he think it would be forever? Did he ever regret it? What had he been doing since then? These were the questions every hardcore fan would have asked. Yet I remembered neither raising them nor the faintest echo of an answer.

Finally I fell into a restless sleep, as one tends to do after a heavy night. When I woke in the afternoon, still hungover, and started to clean up, I discovered that it wasn't only Dylan who had disappeared – my wallet, too, was missing. From what I could remember, I'd last used it, or tried to use it, in the taxi. I must have dropped it either in the car or on the pavement outside. If an honest person found it, I'd get it back. If not, well… I checked what information I needed to cancel my credit card, to be on the safe side, which was about all I could do. Once I'd made the call, I got on with the cleaning.

It was when I hung the guitar back up on the wall that I discovered the third loss. All of Dylan's LP's were gone, from his self-titled debut album to *Blonde on Blonde*. In fact, one more was missing: the double bootleg that I'd sent for after seeing an ad in an *Oz* magazine – Dylan's white album, its sleeve and labels as anonymous as his life had been for almost five decades. Why would he have wanted that? It's true there were some early amateur recordings on it, but almost one third consisted of material from the basement sessions, as they came to be called. And that wasn't his work. I must have insisted that he take it, along with the rest – there was no other explanation. I must have brought them all out and told him how much they'd meant to me. I must have told him that I'd played them until I knew the words and tune of every song of his that had ever been released. Had I also told him about the chaos he created in my life when he chose to leave the scene? I hope not. I hope I left him with nothing but the admiration I still feel today. As long as I did that, I have few regrets. My memories are a lot hazier than I could wish, but they will remain with me always.

That is not to say that the moment never came when I doubted the experience – it was such an extraordinary piece of good luck. Indeed, it took only a day or two before I went in search of the pub for confirmation that it really was Dylan I had met and found myself hopelessly lost in an unfamiliar neighbourhood. The phone directory was of no help: there was a Star Inn, but not in the area where I had been. Still, it's easy to get names wrong, especially on a night of heavy drinking. Not surprisingly, I found no Dark Horse either. In the end I decided not to let it worry me. Whatever the barman might have been able to tell me, he was no expert on Dylan, so what difference would it make? Dustin Hoffman, right? And truly, if I needed proof of some kind of what had occurred, it was there in my own home, staring me in the face, so to speak. It still is – the gap in my record collection. It's the only proof I need. It's a gap that nothing can fill.

Al, if you like.

Bob.

Rejection 1

He deletes the email.

"What did they say?"

"Nothing much. They read it with interest."

"Well, that's something. What else?"

"They enjoyed it."

"Even better. So why so glum?"

"Ultimately they decided it wasn't right for their pages."

"Why?"

"They didn't say."

"Too mundane, I suppose. Who wants to read about us? A nine-to-five life. You need a different subject. That uncle you told me about?"

"What if he found out?"

"How could he? Just change his name."

He hesitates.

"And write in the first person."

He nods.

"That would simplify matters."

"Then get going."

And freed, he does.

Rejection 2

He deletes the email.

"What did they say?"

"Nothing much. They read it with interest."

"Well, that's something. What else?"

"They enjoyed it."

"Even better. So why so glum?"

"Ultimately they decided it wasn't right for their pages."

"Why?"

"They didn't say."

"Too esoteric, I suppose. Abstruse. You should write about us. Ordinary people. A nine-to-five life. That would catch their interest."

"You and me. Using our names?"

"Why not? Nobody would know. And if they did, what of it?"

He hesitates.

"Use the third person."

"Right. That would add some distance."

"Then get going."

And freed, he does.

Rivalry?

The girl behind the library counter yawned. "No card? Got an ID?"

The man shook his head. "I didn't think it would be necessary." He turned to me. "You can vouch for me, can't you?" I must have raised my eyebrows because he added: "Confirm that I'm me."

A harmless plea, if somewhat odd. "Certainly," I said. "If you put it like that."

The girl sighed.

"I'm of the next generation," he told her. He viewed me expectantly.

I sized him up. Younger, yes, if that was what he meant. Well, he needed a name. I'd give him one. "Ron," I suggested. It came out of nowhere.

"Stan."

"Right."

He was waiting.

I followed what I took to be his lead. "Laurel."

He gave a nod.

The girl frowned. "Didn't you say Latimer?"

That rendered merely a shrug. "Laurel. Latimer." He waved as he left, empty-handed.

Latimer. Stan Latimer. If nothing else, I should have recognized his voice. The number of times he has appeared on radio or television in the last decade must exceed that of any other author bar none. And why? Because of his four rewrites of *Great Expectations.* Not much of a feat, I would say. Such things have been done by others and more creatively. I wouldn't hesitate to claim that my own rendition of *Adventures of Huckleberry Finn*, giving the duke the floor, goes far beyond Latimer's paltry efforts. The title itself surpasses anything he has ever accomplished, as does the rape scene that opens the book. You must be familiar with it. "Masterly," declared one reviewer; "a tour de force" was the phrase used by another. I quote: "Pared of adjectives and adverbs, it takes the reader to a point below zero." "Stunningly traumatic," was his conclusion.

It struck me that whilst I hadn't been able to identify him, in view of my past production and the many readings I have given, all around the country, Latimer must have realized who I was. Had he assumed I was being funny? I was, sure enough, but purely in acting on cue. Never mind – I had demonstrated wit, which can hardly be said for his writing. Picking up the book I'd had put on reserve, I followed in his footsteps, wondering what had brought him to my neck of the woods. Had he tired of the north? Well, there should be room for both of us.

Over the next few weeks I came to revise my opinion. Time and again I spotted him from afar, which made me suspect that he was deliberately putting himself in my way. Fortunately, the distance between us was such that I managed to avoid direct contact. What was he doing, wandering around? Were we both in the same fix? I very much doubted it. Personally, I would have gagged on the first volume alone, had I done other than flick through it, but the media would probably swallow any number of renditions of Dickens's novel, regardless of the perspective. Why stop at four, if that was what he was doing, or five, for that matter? Indeed, why not employ a team of writers and play at being in Hollywood. *Great Expectations 6: Startop. Great Expectations 7: The Return of Startop.* No doubt he would enjoy the attention it would generate.

As I hinted, I myself was between books but determined to avoid repetition at any cost – unlike Latimer, I would find the air stale if I were to force a new door open just to get into the same old room. No, I wanted variation. To achieve that, I was waiting for a line that would impress itself upon me – impress itself and thereby release me. The right wording would establish the situation. Along would come an assortment of characters and with them relationships and conflicts. Even though what followed would by no means be plain sailing, the plot would slowly begin to unfold, an open-ended plot, nebulous to start with, but gradually taking shape. Research would close some avenues and open others. This wasn't happening. The words I was seeking were lurking in the shadows, more evasive, perhaps, because of my recent retirement. Freedom from constraints may have brought on its own restraints. In view of my situation, I could have done without Latimer. And it wasn't only in the streets that he disturbed me; at home, too, he squeezed in between me and my work. There I was, squirming at my desk, crossing and uncrossing my feet, and what emerged on the computer screen was neither words nor simply my reflection. No, what returned my look with a smirk wore his features, his blotchy skin – the face he had revealed at our encounter. It bore little resemblance to the photo that graced the volume which endeared him to the media, but then age gets to us all. Not that I would have welcomed the earlier version. His presence would have been equally obnoxious in any shape or form.

"I'm of the next generation," he had stated, taunting me. It was a good thing I didn't catch on. I could have told him a thing or two – as could anyone who values craftsmanship in writing. "Lesson one," we would have asserted, in unison. "Pay heed, young man; you have a lot to learn. Lesson one. Titles and beginnings, in that order, are your major hooks. Bait them with care. Angleworms and maggots will do if the feed store is empty, but they must appear fresh. Your characters needn't, so long as they possess traits that are both lovable and problematic, ideally simultaneously, but your title and beginning must draw the reader in." What would he have made of that?

I had no more than glanced at his first book, of course – no one had asked me to review it – and one reason was that nothing, absolutely nothing in the opening paragraph intrigued me in the least. I reread it, in case there was some level I had missed. There wasn't. Joe's – Pip's brother-in-law's – extended lament evoked no emotions. "Pull yourself together," I wanted to tell him. "It's no major catastrophe. So there were no dogs fighting for veal cutlets at Miss Havisham's? There was no silver basket? What of it?" And I would have made the same remark to Latimer. What of it? I fail to see how anyone could have been tempted to move on, however modest his or her expectations – except to some other book.

I'm not saying writing is easy. A phrase or two that seems highly promising can lead you astray and leave you mired. All that glitters, and so forth. Let me return to the text that some consider my major opus, *What You Know About Me Ain't True*. There, at an early stage, the opening line ran: "When they tar you and feather you and ride you on a rail, you're fetched about as low as you can get." Those were the duke's words. And he went on: "The king died. I didn't." Reviewing those sentences, I flushed with pleasure. My body tingled. I got up, excited to such a degree that I tripped over the cords from my PC and had to grab a standard lamp to break my fall, breaking, instead, the bulb. This was it! Half a day later, and a short one at that, the fizz had gone out of the duke's observation. It was flat. It didn't pull me in. Nor did it open the way for whatever had to follow. On top of that, it could have been factually wrong: it was only in exceptional cases, apparently, that people died from being tarred and feathered. Learning this, I spent days in anguish. Imagine, therefore, how elated I had been as the vision entered my mind, after yet another sleepless night, of the duke being raped as a boy. I'm sure you will recall the scene. I lost myself in the glazed look in his father's eyes. Along with him, I ran my fingers lightly down the exposed skin of the boy's back, stroking his buttock. I breathed in the silence. The tension between father and son mounted while I watched. That introduced complexity.

Complexity, my dear Latimer, is very rarely misplaced.

Three letters aren't likely to attain that. *Joe.* It's on a par with *My Summer Holiday.* Inadequate isn't the word for it.

Oh, I do go on, you say, and I admit I do. It isn't out of envy, though. Far be it from me to question the position Latimer has acquired, irrespective of how. No, what troubles me is a much larger issue and it concerns the poor quality of the stories that hold people captive today. Where will we be one or two generations on? That is what is at stake. And that is why Latimer's face kept cropping up, blocking me, whenever I sat down with the germ of a story.

I had a bank of ideas, naturally, like most writers who take their calling seriously, and had opened the file, attempting to rekindle the enthusiasm I had felt at the time that I put down some fragment or other for future use. It might be of service. The interest might accumulate. That had been my rationale. Sadly, I learned that the opposite was true. Deflation had done its work. That which had appealed to me had faded. The scraps that I reviewed had lost the lustre they once had; exposing them to the light did nothing to restore it.

Growing increasingly despondent as the days went by I would scroll through the entries, the briefest of which read:

"Yours?"
They denied it.

I stared at the two lines. I blinked. What kind of

situation had I envisaged? The exchange was so vague, so unspecific, that it could go anywhere – which, in my present state, was no help whatsoever. Was the reference to a newborn baby bundled up outside the entrance of a hospital? *"Yours?"* Stories of foundlings have their audience. Or was it to a dog that had attacked somebody in the street, tearing clothes and skin? To a car blocking a driveway? The possibilities were endless. I dismissed the entry – actually, I deleted it, as beyond hope.

Once or twice I reckoned I had hit upon something that could do the trick. In one instance I read the passage aloud, breaking off at the end of each line to ponder its impact:

> *He goes over to the window and folds his arms around her.*
> *Outside a car is starting up.*
> *The sound warns him that the temperature has dropped.*
> *There'll be a heavy frost tonight.*

But no frost could keep Latimer at bay; his face rose up in front of me, dimming the text. "And you were the one talking about bait," he sneered. I had to agree. What I had put down had potential only if it was followed without delay by something that would pull the reader in; the unknown is not intriguing in and of itself. In truth, those four lines had the makings of an ending rather than the beginning I was looking for. I asked myself why I had saved pages and pages of such trivia. A child could come up with more tempting alternatives while sucking its dummy.

How long would this go on? I moved around my flat restlessly, sitting down here and there for a different view. My few plants, I saw, empathised. A cyclamen, which I had bought on impulse along with a frozen pizza and some cans of beer, had given up on its new environment. Its leaves yellowed as I stood watching and within hours the bright pink flowers bent, their stems taking on the texture of wet rubber. An African violet, no longer flowering, went next. I reduced watering to a minimum, concentrating on saving two cacti, but in respect of cacti, who can tell how they are doing? With winter approaching, their productivity was probably on a level with mine. I am a cactus, I concluded, but that was no consolation, nor would it attract much attention were I to shout it from the rooftops – or use it for the title of a story.

What put an end to my stay in limbo was something that arrived in the post. Now, brown envelopes of the official kind, as abrasive as the skin on my heels, don't often hold much promise. I was about to toss it on the hall table – some form from the taxman, I assumed, which could wait – when I noticed that the address was handwritten. I turned it over. Scrawled on the back were the words: "This might interest you." There was no signature. Inside – I tore it open – was a flyer where the word RAPE! leapt at me, under a photo of – you guessed it – Latimer, the one from the book that set his career in motion. Below, a reading was announced, in smaller print; the venue, a lecture hall at the university. And that was it. The reverse side was blank. There was nothing to indicate who the sender was.

Ah, he is learning, I decided. *Rape*, to look at the title alone, although he stuck to his one-word formula, was certainly a vast improvement on *Joe* and the rest of his tetralogy. Joyce Carol Oates had gone one better, adding what was, to all appearances, an incongruous subtitle, but you couldn't expect wonders. One step at a time. Who might be the focal character? I'd put my money on Miss Havisham.

I studied the picture. Did Latimer, as is my wont, shy away from photo studios? "Oh, my God," I had muttered, shutting my eyes to what was to adorn the passport I was applying for. "Come, come," the photographer had said. "You look like Cary Grant" – a line she must have memorized for middle-aged men who faulted her work. "Cary Grant dead" would have been an apt rejoinder; "Cary Grant after an untold number of weeks in the grave." Or had Latimer not aged noticeably in the years since the publication of *Joe*? If that was the case, the man who had asked me to confirm his identity must have been someone else. Was he a namesake? An impostor? I flipped the envelope over again for clues that weren't there. Was I the victim of some prank, haunted by the wrong Latimer – or by someone else entirely? The absence of a signature suggested that it could be the latter.

Even so, the phrase pulled me in: "This might interest you." That is what good bait does – in a twinkling, you convince yourself there is no hook hidden in what attracts you. You blink and the sharp point is gone; the eye through which the line has been threaded, should you detect it, becomes at most a minor flaw. If the words were Latimer's, he should have used them as an opener for *Rape*. Perhaps he had. I had half a mind to try and find out – and find out, too, if it was in fact Latimer I had met – and if it was, why he was stalking me – if he was. What had I done to him?

But at a reading?

I pictured him entering the hall. There would be a row of high windows but no view. In semi-darkness – the rays from the sparse fixtures in the ceiling would barely reach the floor – he would walk nimbly towards a lectern, his chin up, and put a book on its sloping top. He would adjust the light, tap on the mike. The murmur from the crowd – students, commanded to be there – would die out. "Chapter one," he would begin. He would examine the audience. "This might interest you."

206

And at the end, there would be a question and answer session. Some of those who raised their hands would be humble, others somewhat strident. "Do you agree with Foucault's claim…" would be expanded into a five-minute monologue. As the speaker in such situations I have learned to adopt a Woody Allen pose, tilting my head from one side to the other, one finger for support. Having caught the final question mark, if there is one, I will say something like, "Could you repeat that, please?" to get the audience on my side, prior to dismissing the matter: "Seriously, there's no given approach to any text. If you consider Foucault helpful, use him. Next?" In many ways, I discovered early on, a performance of this nature resembles a rock concert, where, instead of questions, there are shouted requests. Some of them will be heartfelt and concern material that has a permanent place on the band's set list. One or two will be of the Foucauldian type. A man – always a man – will call for an obscure number from a bootleg or the B-side of a long-forgotten single. What he truly desires is recognition in the form of an appreciative aside or what could be construed as a smile from the star: Ah, a connoisseur! With seasoned performers his wish will be ignored. How would Latimer react? Does he have star quality?

Either way, the show would be unbearable.

My eyes fastened again on the flyer, but it held no secret message. It gave the date, the hour, the venue. All welcome.

I wavered.

Of course, to turn up at an event of this nature entailed no further obligations.

One could leave ahead of question time.

One could leave during the reading itself.

One could make a dramatic exit if one deemed it opportune.

One could.

Could I?

I arrived at to the conclusion that I could.

Thus, on the appointed night, the coldest, wettest, most blustery on record for November this far south, I set off. The wind changed direction constantly, coming now from the east, now from the west, seeking an opening wherever there was a gap between buildings. My anorak gave some protection, but my glasses were exposed, leaving me blinded. Soon my shoes were soaked, as were my trousers to well above the knee. My fingers froze. The prospect of sitting in a lecture hall with my clothes clinging to me was not enticing. Still, I am nothing if not persistent. I was intent on making it there, even if I were to be the entire audience.

I wasn't, though – a scattering of people were already seated when I pushed the door open. With my anorak slung over my arm I made for a seat in the rear, where I would be less conspicuous, accompanied by squeaky sounds, embarrassingly similar to those of an upset stomach. My shoes were acting up. I wiped my glasses. The majority of those present, I noted, were women and, to judge by their age, students. None was a marked Foucauldian. There was no Latimer in sight.

He appeared ten minutes late and a quick glance ascertained that he was the man I had run into at the library. Viewed from a distance, his face was a little less blotched, but our confrontation had been on a Monday morning and he may well have had a rough weekend. Beside him was a woman. She took the few steps over to the lectern while he hung back and once she had tested the microphone, the standard introduction followed. I ticked off the platitudes one by one: "a pleasure to welcome…"; "no presentation should be necessary…"; "who hasn't heard of…" – but switched off the moment she claimed that Latimer had altered the literary map of England. Pinching my right trouser leg between finger and thumb I eased it up a fraction to try to get some air between the material and my skin, but to no avail.

There was a round of applause. The woman was done.

"Good evening," I heard. I leaned forward; Latimer had taken her place. "It's great to see such a big turnout in spite of the weather."

He gave a slight bow after this attempt to magnify the importance of the event and straightened the papers in front of him. It wasn't a book he was about to introduce, then – at least not yet. Was it a set of page proofs he had got from the printer? There weren't enough pages, I would have thought.

He cleared his throat. "Rape," he declared.

I sat back. "No love story, as in Joyce Carol Oates," I mumbled to myself.

"You don't know about me," were his opening words and I must have frowned. He broke off. Was this a chapter heading? I was confused. The phrase was Huck Finn's, not that of some character out of Dickens. To add to my confusion, it became apparent two or three sentences into the text that he had given it to the duke.

"You don't know about me," he repeated, "without you have read a book by the name of *Adventures of Huckleberry Finn*, but that ain't no matter. That book was made by Mr. Mark Twain, and he told the truth, mainly. You may *think* you know me if you run across a book called *What You Know About Me Ain't True*, but it ain't so. *That* book was made by L. F. Roth and ain't nothing but a heap of lies. Worse." He raised his head. His eyes met mine across the hall. "It's an outrage." He paused. "Don't you *believe* that rubbage." Another pause. "There *warn't* no rape. Alas! I *had* no father. He lit out long before I'd learned to crawl, leaving me an orphan with a broken heart."

I had got up from my seat the minute I realized where he was going. RAPE! the flyer had proclaimed, in capitals, quite rightly. It was me being raped. It was my book that was under attack. I felt the audience glare at me as I hurried towards the exit. Latimer had stopped. *Everyone should get out*, was on my lips. *What you're witnessing is an assault! A deliberate provocation!* In my haste I dropped my anorak and had to stoop to pick it up. "Squelch!" went my shoes, punctuating the silence. "Squelch!" No words can describe the turmoil inside of me. My pulse was racing. Letting the door bang shut, I collapsed on a bench in the corridor, out of breath, trembling with rage.

The affront of it.

What I had done with the duke lay entirely within the compass of Mark Twain's creation. This – Latimer's work – was patricide! "I'm of the next generation," he had bragged. Well, I'd show him what the present generation, if I were to accept his claim, thought of his – and at that very instant I perceived how. What had been his contribution to English literature? Nothing of the least import. *Joe*, *Biddy*, *Wemmick*, and *Molly* – or was it *Nelly*? Four slim volumes doomed to collect dust in library depots. And now he was taking on the duke. Not even Twain's duke. Mine. *Rape.* I'd give him rape.

I brought out my notebook. Ignoring what might be going on inside the lecture hall, I groped for my pen for the first time in weeks. No sound seeped out to distract me. Were they, each and every one, as attentive to their business as I was to mine? The scene that had arisen before my inner eye held me, observer and participant both. The phrases tumbled over one another, much as they had been spoken. I had to do little more than set them down. They needed no reflection or embellishment.

When, presently, I came to a halt, it wasn't for want of

210

ideas. I knew what direction to take. I knew some feasible stops. Pleased I read through my jottings, tapping the rhythm with my pen:

The girl behind the library counter yawned. "No card?"

I pulled on my anorak and, having struggled briefly with the zip, headed out into the rain.

The girl...

This promised to be good. Everything was there, in my mind, fighting for space. Characters. Setting. Plot. Just you wait, Latimer! Just you wait! I'll let you see who is the master.

The girl behind the library counter yawned.

No. Strike that.

The girl behind the counter shot a glance at him. "No card?" Her hands left the keyboard. She yawned. "Got an ID? Unless you produce some..." She let the words hang in the air; I don't know you from Adam, they implied.

I smiled and quickened my pace. The wind, the rain, the cold no longer bothered me. I was no longer between books! I was finally going somewhere!

The girl behind the counter shot a glance at him. "No card?" Her hands, as graceful as those of a ballet dancer, left the keyboard. She yawned. "Got an ID? Got an ID? Got an ID...?"

It was not until I got home that it struck me that Latimer's whole arrangement may well have been intended as a practical joke. Stan Laurel, I had called him when we met in the library, as if I considered him a comedian. I'll

211

show you, he may have thought – he obviously didn't realize that I hadn't recognized him. A joke would be a fitting form of retaliation. For surely he wouldn't waste time writing a book about one of the characters in Huck Finn simply to annoy me. There'd be nothing in it for him. If he was giving a course at the university, as seemed likely, it wouldn't take long to set things up. He'd have to prepare an invite for me – I'd seen none elsewhere, not even on the door to the lecture hall. His students could have been informed in class. "A mock reading," he could have explained, so they would be prepared for what followed. The person who introduced him probably was a colleague. As for the text he was to read from, a page or two would suffice – after that, he could break off to let me know that he'd been having me on: there was no book in the making. I shook my head. I would find out in time, I suppose. If no book appeared, that was it.

Either way, it had got me going – which was good enough for now. That mattered more than anything else. Right?

Acknowledgements

"Dance?", "The Race" and "Love" first published by Earlyworks Press in *The Ball of the Future: Stories Long and Short*, 2016.

"Detroit" first published by The Plymouth Writers Group in *Secrets & Lies*, 2017.

"Cleaning Windows in the Dark" first published by Biscuit Publishing in *International Prize-Winning Stories and Poetry*, 2011.

"Going on Eighty-Six" first published by Momaya Press in *Momaya Short Story Review, Ambition.* 2016.

"Episode" first published by Bridge House Publishing in *Snowflakes*, 2015.

"Cat in the Snow" first published by Bridge House Publishing in *Light in the Dark*, 2014.

"Scene: Another Part of the Island" first published by Earlyworks Press in *The Ball of the Future: Stories Long and Short*, 2016.

"This Is for You" first published by Cinnamon Press in *The Day I Met Vini Reilly & Other Stories*, 2016.

"loss.doc" first published by Earlyworks Press in *Barcelona to Bihar: Stories That Travel With You*, 2012.

"What Is There to Say?" first published by University of Huddersfield Press in *I You He She It: Experiments in Viewpoint*, 2017.

"In the Year of the Summer of Love (Elsewhere)" and "The Sound of Patriarchy" first published by Earlyworks Press in *Significant Spaces*, 2013.

"No Bear" first published by Bridge House Publishing in *Baubles: An Anthology*, 2016.

"Only Sometimes" and "The Real Thing" first published by Earlyworks Press in *The Several Deaths of Finbar's Father & Other Stories*, 2014.

"Moe" first published by Bridge House Publishing in *Glit-er-ary: An Anthology*, 2017.

My thanks go to the jurors and editors, especially at Bridge House Publishing, who made this publication possible.

About the Author

L. F. Roth has had a varied working life, consisting, in England, of a few years in residential child care and as a ward orderly; in the U.S., of a year's research in American literature; and in Sweden, of work as a translator, teacher and university lecturer. There, in the 1980s, he published an award-winning book for children with reading difficulties, which was later translated into Danish and Norwegian.

Some twenty-five of his short stories have appeared in competition anthologies in the UK, many of them reprinted in this volume.

Like to Read More Work Like This?

Then sign up to our mailing list and download our free collection of short stories, *Magnetism*. Sign up now to receive this free e-book and also to find out about all of our new publications and offers.

Sign up here:
   http://eepurl.com/gbpdVz

Please Leave a Review

Reviews are so important to writers. Please take the time to review this book. A couple of lines is fine.

Reviews help the book to become more visible to buyers. Retailers will promote books with multiple reviews.

This in turn helps us to sell more books… And then we can afford to publish more books like this one.

Leaving a review is very easy.

Go to https://smarturl.it/97cgcv, scroll down the left-hand side of the Amazon page and click on the "Write a customer review" button.

Read More of L.F Roth's Work in These Books

Cat in the Snow in
Light in the Dark
Published by Bridge House (2014)

    Order from Amazon:

    Paperback: ISBN 978-1-907335-37-2
    eBook: ISBN 978-1-907335-38-9

Episode in
Snowflakes
Published by Bridge House (2015)

    Order from Amazon:

    Paperback: ISBN 978-1-907335-40-2
    eBook: ISBN 978-1-907335-41-9

No Bear in
Baubles
Published by Bridge House (2016)

    Order from Amazon:

    Paperback: ISBN 978-1-907335-46-4
    eBook: ISBN 978-1-907335-47-1

Moe in
Glit-er-ary
Published by Bridge House (2017)

    Order from Amazon:

    Paperback: ISBN 978-1-907335-55-6
    eBook: ISBN 978-1-907335-56-3

Other Publications by Bridge House

Fresh Beginnings

by Leela Dutt
illustrated by Kate Attfield

An intriguing mixture of stories, all in Leela Dutt's inimitable style – something here for everyone, and beautifully illustrated by Kate Attfield.

Some are short and funny, some poignant – Leela Dutt's collection *Fresh Beginnings* will warm your heart and stay in your mind – it might even make you laugh!

"If you like short stories, if you like good stories, then *Fresh Beginnings* is for you." (*Amazon*)

Order from Amazon:

Paperback: ISBN 978-1-914199-12-7
eBook: ISBN 978-1-914199-13-4

What If...

by Anne Wilson

"What if?" An unanswered question. The unexplained, a mystery, a road not taken. This is a collection of dark fiction injected here and there with glimmers of humour.

The author takes us on a surreal and ghostly journey from Latin America's Day of the Dead, through the coastal towns of Lancashire, a pig farm in Denmark, a high-rise in Mallorca, a haunted vicarage at Christmas and a town centre coffee bar. The voices we hear are variously plaintive, nostalgic, and occasionally vindictive or vengeful: the testimonies and fears of the living and the dead.

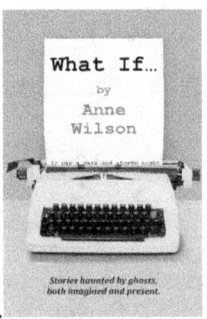

"The author weaves a thrilling web with her prose, creating delightful pocket worlds to entice and entrance the reader. These are stories that linger long in the mind after reading." (*Amazon*)

Order from Amazon:

Paperback: ISBN: 978-1-914199-14-1
eBook: 978-1-914199-15-8

Speculations

by Stephen Faulkner

What if?

All good stories and novels begin very simply when the author asks the question, "What if…?" In the fourteen stories in Speculations the author offers each solution while leaving it up to you to figure out the "what if…?" question that each tale alludes to.

Each story is an intriguing journey into the realms of imagination, fantasy and the incredible. Some of the places you will be taken in this book include the inner mind of a creature that remains on Earth long after the human race has been eliminated; a world that exports a tasty treat that originates in a quite unsavoury place; and an all-knowing, all powerful alien machine which can do literally anything at all.

Order from Amazon:

Paperback: ISBN: 978-1-914199-08-0
eBook: 978-1-914199-09-7

www.ingramcontent.com/pod-product-compliance
Lightning Source LLC
Chambersburg PA
CBHW061146170626
46809CB00003B/1000